On All Hallows' Eve

Weekly Reader Books presents

On All Hallows' Eve
Grace Chetwin

Lothrop, Lee & Shepard Books • New York

This book is a presentation of *Weekly Reader Books.*
Weekly Reader Books offers book clubs for children from
preschool through high school. For further information write
to: **Weekly Reader Books,** *4343 Equity Drive, Columbus,*
Ohio 43228

Edited for Weekly Reader Books and published by arrangement
with Lothrop Lee & Shepard Books.

Cover illustrated by David Wenzel.
Cover copyright © 1987 by Field Publications.
Text copyright © 1984 by Grace Chetwin.

Library of Congress Cataloging in Publication Data
Chetwin, Grace. On All Hallows' Eve. Summary: Two sisters
on their way home from a Halloween party step into another
time period, where the forces of good and evil involve them in
a life-or-death adventure. [1. Space and time—Fic-
tion. 2. Fantasy] I. Title.
PZ7.C425550n 1984 [Fic] 84-4391 ISBN 0-688-03012-2

For
Claire & Briony
who have been there

For
Barbara
who asked

And with thanks
to all who listened and had their say
especially to
Sallie & Briony

But there is no
road through the woods.

                    Rudyard Kipling

One

The two girls trudged along Horse Hollow Road in their Halloween costumes, the cold from Long Island Sound at their backs.

Meg scuffed the dying, drying leaves along the way, flicking them to her left across her sister's path, waiting . . .

Under the yellow streetlight, their breath

made little round clouds, teasing clouds that danced ahead of them, then dissolved like will-o'-the-wisps. Meg opened her mouth and blew out hard, watching the little puff of vapor curl away. Yes, she thought, like will-o'-the-wisps— or speech balloons in a comic strip. A comic strip called *Red Riding Hood Bugs the Baby Witch*. All she needed were words for Sue's balloons—words that should be coming any minute now . . .

She flicked the leaves again and, at last, her trick paid off.

"Meg! Cut it out!" Holding onto her witch's hat, Sue pushed past Meg and crossed the road. "Just because *you* don't want to go to the party, there's no need to take it out on me!"

Meg laughed in triumph. She saw her sister's words, peppered with asterisks and exclamation points, dancing in front of Sue's baby face. How easy it was to get Sue's goat!

Still, Meg was glad of an excuse to cross the road, for there was something about that part of Horse Hollow that gave her the creeps.

She looked back over her shoulder and shivered, as though cold fingers had touched the nape of her neck. She always shivered when she saw that broken-down fence and the ruined cottage behind it. She could not say why, but they filled her with a strong sense of foreboding. A cold came from that place, even in warm sunlight—and it had been really warm when they had come to Locust Valley early in September, a month or so before.

Of course, she had not wanted to leave England.

"You'll like it in the States, you'll see," Father had told her.

"But school's only just started!"

"Believe it or not, they have schools over there too," Father had replied. "And since when did you like the one you're at now? Come on, Meg, face it. Wherever you've gone, you've been unhappy and fighting inside a week!"

"That's not true! I've just started Latin classes with Mrs. Drew, and she says I'm off to a good start."

Father had laughed then, the laugh that said that Meg would not get her way this time.

"I won't go, I won't!" she had told herself over and over every night in bed. She had even tried to make a pact with Sue to run away, but baby Sue had refused. "Oh, well. I shall just go off to Wales by myself until they've all gone, and then Gran and Grandad Jenkins will have to take care of me."

But she hadn't gone off, and here she was, in

glorious Locust Valley, on Long Island, U.S.A. She thought about the kids she'd left behind in England. Even the ones she'd really disliked were better than the ones here. She hated the way they stared at her, and the way they laughed at how she spoke. The only thing worse was the way the grown-ups gushed. "What a cute accent," they said, every time she opened her mouth. Oh, she could *spit!*

She kicked savagely at a fallen branch and ran up behind Sue.

How Sue waddles when she is mad, Meg thought. Like Donald Duck! And how crazy her hair looks, flying out like that around the rim of her pointy hat. It flared to bright yellow under the streetlight. Like a halo—or an undercooked doughnut! Meg laughed aloud.

Sue had Father's silky blonde hair, of course, not the wiry black thatch she'd gotten from Mother. Like brambles, it was, especially under the brush. Sue had Father's round pink English face, too, while she herself had a dark thin Welsh face—a Celtic face, so Mother said.

"Remember you're a Celt, and a Jenkins, like me. And that is why you are called Myfanwy, after Gran Jenkins, and Gwyneth, for Great-Aunt Jones." *Myfanwy* meant "my fine one," as Mother told her again and again.

But even in kindergarten, her name had brought her nothing but trouble. "They won't say it right," she told her mother. "They call me 'Miffie' and laugh when I get mad." Day after day she came home crying, until Mother went into school to tell the teacher to call her by a new name: *Meg*, taking the *M* from Myfanwy and the *G* from Gwyneth. Even then it was a long time before the children changed from "Miffie" to "Meg."

"Never mind," Mother had consoled her. "One day you won't be in school any longer, and then you'll be proud of your names." And Mother would tell Meg wonderful stories about old Wales to cheer her up, especially about Morgan le Fay, King Arthur's witch sister.

"Do you think her blood is in us, Mother?" Meg would ask.

"Perhaps," Mother always said. "Perhaps."

Not that anybody in Locust Valley could care about Meg's Celtic blood, or Morgan le Fay. At least the kids back in England had asked her to tell them stories sometimes, in the lunch line or out on the playground, and for a while she would feel all warm, and part of things. But these kids thought her strange to be talking about such matters—especially that big bully Kenny Stover.

13

From the first he had mocked her accent loudly in front of the others. And when he had overheard her trying to tell about how Morgan le Fay had given King Arthur his sword, Excalibur, Kenny really had shown his dislike. "Hey, come off it, you guys," he'd said. "Quit listening to that stuff. That Wilson kid's too weird!"

Wilson! Meg sighed. Well, at least he'd never heard of *Miffie!* She had watched him swagger off down the hall, longing to pay him back. But she hadn't—yet. If she ever heard him coming down the corridor, she would dodge around the corner and not come out until he had gone.

Now to make things worse, he'd found out about her violin.

It was all Mother's fault.

In spite of Meg's protests, Mother had stormed the principal's office on the first day and got her extra time off from school to practice. As a consequence, she had had to play for the whole school in assembly last week. Since then, there had been no holding Kenny Stover.

Now whenever he saw her, he would swing an imaginary fiddle up onto his shoulder and make the strangest whining noises somewhere up his nose. Of course, everybody laughed and avoided her now as if she had the plague. Oh, bother Kenny Stover and her violin!

"But it's not Kenny really," Sue told her. "And it's not the violin either. It's you. You act so stuck up. Sallie Carpenter leaves to practice ice-skating four days a week, and no one minds her."

Meg sighed again. Even her own sister turned against her when the chips were down. More than ever she wanted to run away somehow, back to Gran and Grandad Jenkins.

"Hey—Sue! Mother told us to stick together!" Shifting her Red Riding Hood basket onto one arm, Meg snatched at Sue's black witch's shawl—Mother's favorite evening shawl, actually.

But Sue shook her off in a rare fit of independence. "She also said a lot of other things—not that they'll make much difference to you."

"Oh, just listen to her: differrrrence, differrrrrence." Meg rolled the *r's* to the point of absurdity. "You should just hear yourself." She drew alongside Sue. "You don't sound American at all. And you don't sound English anymore, either. You don't sound like anything."

"I do so," Sue cried, forced at last to slow her pace. Too many crisps and toffees, Father said. *Potato chips* and *candy* they called them here. Meg made a face. Would she ever get it straight? Sue had already. She always managed to land on her little pink feet. Why, she had even wormed her way into the fifth grade instead of the fourth where she belonged. If Sue could have gotten into Meg's sixth grade class, she would have, Meg was sure. And friends! Sue had so many friends already!

But she doesn't have everything, Meg comforted herself. She doesn't have my long skinny legs. She can't even *squeeze* into my jeans. And she can't run for miles and miles as I can without getting out of breath.

The girls went on in silence. The malicious amusement faded slowly from Meg's face, leaving her features pinched and sullen under the bright red hood.

They reached the T-junction with Bayville Road.

Meg had not wanted to go to this stupid party thing, but Mother, doing a real Mother this time, had literally pushed her through the front door.

"Go on out," she'd said. "Mix, make friends. And don't come home until at least half past eight!"

"Let *her* go!" Meg had yelled back. "She's the one that's so popular! She's the one with all the friends!"

But Mother had already closed the front door in her face.

"Mix, my eye," Meg grumbled to herself. "It's all right for her, staying at home all the time, writing, with editors' deadlines as an excuse. How many friends has *she* made? She should try practicing what she preaches, for a change. How would *she* like to have to sit on her own in the schoolyard, or having to run the risk of meeting Kenny Stover at any minute?"

A brisk wind along Bayville Road caught the rim of Sue's hat. It was so cold. But it was only ordinary cold, not like the cold by the ruined cottage fence. Just the thought of it made Meg shudder.

Strung across Bayville Road by the school gate, a sagging banner dripped mist beads down onto the street. Meg could not read the letters clearly in the darkness, but she knew what they said:

Halloween Party
Mystery Barrel, Bobbing for Apples,
Bazaar, Costume Parade
AND
Hayrides
October 31, from 7 to 10 P.M.

As Meg and Sue drew closer, they could see the arc lights flooding the playing field and clusters of silhouetted figures hurrying toward it. Faint canned music throbbed on the air.

17

Catching the excitement in spite of herself, Meg quickened her pace. Maybe out of the regular school routine, things would be better. Maybe in all the fun, someone would talk to her. And maybe, *maybe* Kenny Stover might not be there—or if he were, he might not make her look foolish in front of everyone.

Yes, it might be all right, she told herself. It might not be so bad after all. . . .

Two

The bazaar was in the auditorium. They went in and bought caramel apples. All of the kids in Meg's sixth grade class were there, laughing and chattering, but not one of them even looked at her. Meg gazed around the room. The whole busy scene was a bright shop window full of good things, and there she was, with her nose pressed up against the cold dark glass, not knowing how to get in.

She went outside again, Sue following, to lean against a corner of the main building, licking her apple, and watching them all have their fun.

Sue moved away from the wall, shivering.

"Come on, Meg," she said. "I'm freezing. Let's move."

"Move where?"

"Oh—I don't know. Let's—bob for apples. It's warmer in a crowd."

"Ugh." Meg made a face, but she followed Sue all the same back into the light.

"Hi, Sue!" somebody called.

Sue turned. "Oh, hi," she said. The passing imp knocked off her hat with a friendly fist.

"Cheek," Meg declared loudly. "He needs a good punch on the nose."

"Shut up, shut *up*!" Sue whispered fiercely. She snatched up her hat and marched off. Meg followed her to the tail of the apple barrel line, mimicking her.

"Hey, Sue!"

"Oh, lor," Meg said.

A bunch of fifth graders came up behind them.

"C'm'ere." A girl grabbed Sue's sleeve. "My dad's running the hay rides, and he's treating us all to a ride around the block." She tugged at Sue's arm. Sue looked at Meg.

"Oh, don't mind me." Meg turned away.

"You'll still be here when I get back?"

Meg shrugged. "Maybe."

There was a brief, awkward pause until, with a whoop, her classmates swept Sue away, exploding into loud laughter as they moved out of the front gate. Meg watched them run across Ryefield Road and onto the playing field where the horse and hay cart waited.

They were laughing at her, Meg was sure. And Sue was joining in. Well, she should care.

Suddenly, it was her turn to duck.

There were four barrels, or rather large, rectangular troughs, standing neat as a slab of chocolate bar. She looked down, saw the fat red apples bob-bobbing in the dark water, saw the wet faces coming up, glistening and sheepish. How grotty the water must be with all those people slobbering into it, and how cold their faces must feel now.

She stepped quickly out of line, slipped her hood back over her head, and paused, irresolute, missing Sue now. She felt so self-conscious out there all alone.

At that moment she heard a weird, thin

whining, an all-too-familiar sound, like that of a mosquito with a bellyache—or Kenny Stover making noises up inside his nose.

She half turned, her heart sinking. Yes, there he was, right across from her on the other side of the barrels, thinly disguised as Dracula and sawing away on an invisible violin.

Meg glanced around.

Everyone was staring.

She wanted to move away, but she could not. Kenny knew that she had seen him. Out of the corner of her eye, she watched him stop with a flourish and a bow. There was loud applause mixed with catcalls, from a bunch of tall, broad devils, a gorilla, and a skeleton. Kenny's buddies from the junior high where he should have gone this year!

Behind Kenny, to his left, clung his inevitable kid brother, Rip, a first grader, dressed as E.T. She closed her eyes. Now that little wimp was going to ask for an encore, as he always did when he was around.

"Encore, encore," Rip cried. Meg could cheerfully have rammed the words down his scraggy little throat!

Kenny obliged by bowing again.

Now he would ape her English accent, and say, "And now for may grend fee-nah-lee: The

Flaight of the Bumble Bee!" Then he would hoist the imaginary fiddle back up onto his shoulders, and start the mosquito noise again.

As she stood listening to the laughter, her face burning, she had suddenly had enough: of Kenny, of the school, of everyone. Elbowing her way through the lines to the other side of the water troughs, she put her hand flat on Kenny's back, and pushed with all her might.

For one moment he stood there, an astonished look on his vampire face; then, caught off balance, he tottered and fell, fangs first, with a splash, among the apples.

In the silence, she walked away.

"Hey! Hey—you! Wilson!" Kenny's voice was angry. She did not look back. She made herself walk with dignity to the corner of the school building, where, once out of sight, she hoisted her Red Riding Hood skirts and ran.

Three

She locked herself in a stall in the girls' washroom, leaned against the wall, and stared blindly at "Mary likes Steve," and "Mrs. Jellicoe stinks." Now she'd done it, for sure. That bully, that hunk of— lout! He'd kill her, in plain sight of them all. She could see the headlines: *Slaughter in the Sixth Grade. Enraged Youth Strangles Helpless English Girl. Bystanders Look On.*

Oh, why had she done it? She could hear Father now:

"You stick your neck out, Meg, and then you are surprised when you get it chopped."

And look where she'd stuck it this time: right under Kenny Stover's nose. The whole school thought twice about crossing that bully—the dummy, having to repeat sixth grade!

She crossed her arms tightly as she always did when in a fix, frowning and rocking herself from side to side.

Now what? Oh, where was Sue? Trust the girl not to be around when she was needed!

Long minutes passed.

Then there was a sudden flurry. It was time for the costume parade. Outside in the passage, noises swelled and died.

Meg listened to the sudden quiet, her hope rising. Maybe she could dodge out now while everyone was over on the playing field watching the parade. She could go through the side gate and wait for Sue along Horse Hollow Road.

She opened the stall door and crept out. Her hair was a mess, and her painted cheeks had smudged up around her eyes, giving her a feverish look, but too bad about that.

She opened the outer door a slit.

The hallway was deserted.

To her right, the passage led to the front hall

and entrance overlooking Ryefield Road and the playing field. To her left, it led to a side door and a little gate onto Bayville Road. Meg turned left.

She made it all the way to the side gate, and was just slipping through when a shadow moved out from the gatepost.

"Well, well, well." Kenny grabbed for her basket. "What have we here?" Meg let go—left him holding Mother's brand-new fruit basket—and ran back into school, through the long, bright corridors, past the auditorium to the front hall, and out through the door.

The school yard was empty. Straight across from her, people were sitting in the bleachers watching a single line of witches and goblins and E.T.'s and monsters and ghosts parading around a roped-off arena.

Meg peered around cautiously. Perhaps Kenny had given up and gone over to the parade. Should she try for the front gate? She edged out into the light.

"Meg?" A witch emerged from the trees bordering the drive and ran toward her. "Oh, Meg! I've been looking all over!"

Sue came panting up. "Oh, Meg, whatever has been going on? They say Kenny Stover is out to get you!"

"He is, and will, if you don't stop bellowing my name all over the place! Come on!"

They made for the front gate and were almost there when the skeleton and the gorilla from the junior high stepped out to block their way. Without a word, both girls started back for the main building.

"Quick! In here!" Meg dodged into the auditorium, which was still crammed with booths from the bazaar. Through it they ran, toward the doors at the far end. They were about halfway there when those doors burst open. Kenny stood with his arms outspread. The skeleton and the gorilla ran in behind them, cutting off their line of retreat.

Sue squealed. There was no way out.

"Here!" Meg ran for the steps leading up onto the stage.

"But it's out-of-bounds tonight!"

So what, Meg thought, taking the steps two at a time. Sue followed anyway, as Meg made for the stage side door leading back out into the corridor. It was locked! Now they really were trapped!

She turned and, hearing feet pounding up the stage steps, backed against the wall.

Suddenly, there was a shout from below.

"Here! You boys! Come back here!"

27

The footsteps stopped abruptly.

"You were told this morning about not going up there tonight, *and* you were told the penalty for disobeying! Take off your masks and let's have names!"

Meg peered out onto the stage.

The principal was standing at the foot of the steps with his back to her, writing in a little notebook.

Her knees shaking, Meg tiptoed down and past them all, Sue at her heels. As she passed Kenny, he whispered, "You won't get far, Wilson. I'll get you double for this!"

Outside, Sue cried, "Oh, Meg. Kenny looked really mad!"

As if Meg needed Sue to tell her that!

"You stay here," she said. "I'll send Mother for you. Me, I'm going to have to move." With that, Meg turned and made for the front door, running for her life!

Four

In spite of Meg's words, Sue tagged along.

Was Kenny on his way? Meg dearly wanted to look. But she didn't. Her father was a champion runner. "Never look back," he had told her so often. "It slows you up and gives your rival the edge." And so she didn't, all the way along Bayville Road. But at the T-junction with Horse

Hollow, the temptation was too great. After all, why run if Kenny was not even following them?

So she did look and was so surprised at what she saw that she actually stopped to watch.

The boys were there all right, but they were just standing down the road a way, shouting and waving their arms about. A moment later, the devils, the gorilla, and the skeleton turned and headed back to the party, leaving the vampire and E.T. behind.

The vampire turned and saw her. Bother! If he'd been going to quit and follow his buddies Meg realized he couldn't afford to now.

"Hey—Wilson! I'm coming! Watch out!" He began to run.

Meg started after Sue, catching up with her and passing her with ease. But from then on Sue kept at her heels, puffing like an old steam train. Even at that moment, Meg felt an old familiar resentment. She, Meg, was supposed to be the runner.

On they ran. Meg could almost feel Kenny's hand on her arm. Her father's warning came again: *Never look back.* Easier said than done.

Ahead, a high mercury vapor light signaled the corner of their street, Millford Drive. Kenny would never dare follow them that far.

Just as Meg was beginning to think that they

would be safe. Sue pulled her toward the fence, shouting, "He's here!"

Now Meg squealed. She had been so busy being frightened of Kenny that she had not noticed where they were. Sue was actually drawing her toward the strange cold of the ruined cottage!

"No! Ow, Sue! Let go! I don't want to go in there!"

Meg struggled hard, the chill of the place at once drawing and repelling her. Goosebumps started up her arms. But fight as she may, she found Sue's grip surprisingly firm. "He'll get you if you don't come quick. Here, mind that nail, and—ouch! there's another!"

Meg clung vainly to a piece of rotten railing only to have it come away in her hand. She half fell through the gap, and there she was, standing in front of the cottage.

"But I don't *like* it here!" Meg felt the hysteria rising inside her. She looked toward the darkness of the cottage behind the overgrown bushes. "There're rats and goodness knows what in there."

The crash of Kenny's boots through the leaves out along the winding path drew nearer.

Sue was shaky with fear. "Meg—please—into the cottage before he sees us."

Meg dug in her heels but Sue won the day. In the next minute, Meg was being pushed and pulled from the fence, across crunchy pebbles, and over a rotted doorsill.

They were inside.

"This is ridiculous," Meg whispered fiercely, shifting her fear of the place onto her fear of Kenny. "He's bound to guess where we've gone."

They edged further in from the doorway, out across the floor. It creaked ominously in places, and once Meg put her foot clean through the rotting planks. Then she nudged an unseen bottle with her toe. It rolled away to clink loudly against something metal.

There was silence.

This was worse, much worse, Meg decided, than the running.

The stink of the place was foul: it was a mixture of ripe refuse, little dead things, and mold, and mildew, and goodness knows what else.

Meg began to feel sick.

Sue's voice came in her ear. "There's another door through the far side. If we can get out there, there's a path that'll take us to Dr. Greaves's back fence—he lives opposite us, you know, about three doors down."

"Oh? How do you know?"

There was a slight pause. "I came through here last Tuesday."

"Aha! So that's how you got home first! Big deal!"

On that day, Meg had gone home without Sue, only to find that Sue had somehow managed to arrive first. Meg, annoyed, had accused her of begging a ride from someone.

"No I didn't," Sue had insisted. "And, anyway, what if I did? There's no law that says I can't!"

That had triggered a really bad fight that had lasted right through the next day.

Meg listened. There was still no sound from beyond the ruined walls. Was Kenny waiting out on the road, or had he followed them in? Was he listening for them out front, or was he creeping around the outside of the cottage to catch them as they went out the back?

Close by, an owl hooted.

Crash! Meg bumped into an empty gasoline can, which made her start and crack her head against a doorpost. Furious, she smashed it with her fist, only to hit an old bolt. "Ow!"

"Sshh!" Sue took her arm. "Here, this way."

"All right, all *right*!" Meg shook her off. The fact that Sue had already been through here once didn't make her the boss.

Meg took two or three tentative steps through the inner doorway. Ahead was an even thicker darkness: the darkness of outside. "Sue . . .

Sue . . ." Oh, where was she! Something horrid touched Meg's mouth. She raised her hand in panic and pulled off a wad of cobweb. "Sue! Sue! Where *are* you?"

"Here, Meg. Over here."

"Over where?"

Before Sue could answer, Meg's whole body began to tingle as though sparks were running up and down it. There was an odd *burnt* smell as the air around her flared into a cold brilliance, lighting up that desolate ruin. Sue was by the outer doorway, and Meg was just through the inner one. The whole scene was vivid, yet drained of color as though they stood frozen in a lightning flash.

The brightness dimmed to a brownish yellow, like the old snapshots of Gran and Grandad Jenkins and Great-Aunt Gwyneth. Then everything went hazy until Meg couldn't see anything but the light. When the haze cleared, the old ruin was gone, and Meg found herself standing instead in a homely kitchen lit by oil lamps that hung from rough-hewn beams.

Five

Meg blinked once or twice, but that was all. She had never believed the things that people did in books when such things happened to them—like stand open-mouthed saying feeble stuff like, *Oh, my,* and *wow.*

An old woman stood before a large black stove stirring a large round pot. She was very fat, and her clothes made her look fatter. She wore a wide patched skirt down to her black button boots, and a blue-and-white checked apron that matched the curtains at the window. The thick brown shawl over her shoulders looked as though it had been made from an old army blanket—one that had seen a few campaigns.

Sue was still standing by the kitchen doorway, her mouth open wide.

"Oh, my," Sue said. And, "Wow."

Meg rolled her eyes ceilingward in disgust.

The old woman finished stirring, set down the spoon, and turned around.

What a jolly face she has, Meg thought. The old woman smiled broadly, as though she welcomed witches and Red Riding Hoods into her kitchen every day.

"Well, sit down. Supper's done. You like stew?"

To her surprise, Meg found herself and Sue reaching for chairs from under the little scrubbed table in the middle of the room. As they sat, they stared at the checked curtains, the neat stitched *Home Sweet Home* hanging on the wall, the open cupboard crammed with cups and plates and pots and pans, and a great flatiron— a real antique, if only the black enamel on the back of it weren't so shiny and new. Behind the kitchen door on a stout wooden peg hung a caped greatcoat and several long scarves. Rag rugs lay like stepping stones on the scoured tiles.

The rotten smell was gone. The air now reeked of beeswax, kitchen soap, and freshly ironed sheets. Over all, though, rose the thick tang of stew, every bit as mouthwatering as Gran Jenkins's. Gran Jenkins always cooked her stew over her old Welsh coal stove, dismissing "those new-fangled electric and gas contraptions" as "the foolish tools to strip good food of its taste."

But that was Gran Jenkins's choice.

There was no electricity or gas in this place, and Meg was sure in some strange way that the old woman had heard of neither.

Meg stared across the table at Sue. How silly she looked, gaping around at everything like a baby. Meg took the spoon that the old woman gave her and scooped up the hot gravy. It burned her mouth. She glanced at Sue. Sue was carefully blowing on hers before putting it gingerly to her lips.

"Well, well." The old woman crossed her arms under her bosom with satisfaction. "Now isn't that putting the warm back in?" Her face curved upward into a jolly smile. She drew out a third chair and sat facing Meg, her elbows on the table. "I don't suppose," she said, "that either of you has seen my boy?"

Meg stared. "Your . . . boy?"

The old woman pointed to the kitchen door. "Out there. He's been gone pretty long. I've been waiting and waiting, but he ha'n't showed up." Her jolly face grew anxious.

Meg caught Sue's eye and shrugged. None of this could be real, she decided. None of it, not even the stew.

"It was the toffee apples, I bet," she murmured.

"*Caramel* apples, you mean." Sue corrected her. "Anyway, what was?"

Meg waved her hand around. "That did all this, silly. I'll bet it was George Merrill. Or that Doug Shawn. I bet they stuck something in the toffee apples to trip us out."

Sue's face twisted into disbelief. "That isn't true, Meg. You're making up stories again." Her face cleared. "And, anyway, if we're . . . tripping out . . . how come we're both on the same trip?"

Warming to her theory, Meg dismissed Sue's question. "It has to be that. We both know that this kitchen can't be real. These walls are all fallen in. *That's* real. The roof"—she looked up at the rough-hewn beams overhead—"that's long gone. And the doors and the floor. And that old woman . . . look at her . . . she can't be real, either."

"But she's *here*," Sue said. "And so is this stew, and I'm getting quite full on it. Explain that."

Meg dropped her spoon into her empty bowl with a clatter. "Oh, you really are gone, Sue. The answer is simple if you would only think. We're probably both lying here—there—in the middle of this—that ghastly floor—in all that stink, spaced out and catching our deaths of cold. We'll likely *be* dead by the time they find us—especially if Kenny finds us first."

"Oh, Meg, don't!"

"Such a good boy," the old woman went on. "For all that they say. Me, I know it takes one good man to reckonerise another, and if there's his match around here, I ha'n't seen him. Now, keep an eye out for him, all right? Tell him his poor ma's keeping the lamp lit and the pot hot, and to hurry on home."

The smiley lines in her homely face drooped, leaving it unutterably sad.

Meg surveyed her empty bowl. For imaginary stew, it had certainly hit the spot.

"What do you call your son?" she asked.

"Tom. Tom Baldry."

Baldry. Baldry. She hadn't heard of any Baldry. Which wasn't saying much. She knew hardly anyone. But what was she thinking of? Hadn't she just said this woman was not real? "How old is he?"

"I can't exackerly say, not now. It's been a while. But he was twenty-eight years old when I last saw him. Twenty-eight years, and three months, and four days." The old woman sighed. "Times I've gone over to that door to put on my coat and go out to look for him, but somehow something's always gotten in my way."

Meg pushed back her chair and stood up. "Come on, Sue."

Sue stood and slid her chair back under the table with great care. "Thank you, Mrs. Baldry." She picked up the empty soup bowls.

"Mother Baldry's the name. Just leave them dishes be. Thank you, anyways. You're a real good gal." She did not look at Meg. "Just go on now. Go on, for you've a ways to go."

"A *ways*?" Meg stopped, her hand on the door latch. It was only a few feet to Sue's precious back fence. But before she could say this, the light flared and dimmed again, leaving them in pitch dark. The smell of wax and clean linen and stew was gone.

Somehow, Meg realized, they were back in the ruined cottage. The old sick feeling returned at the stench in that place. Yet the warmth in her belly remained.

"Oh, well," she said.

Kenny's voice came in answer. "Wilson? Wilson? I hear you. Watch out—here I come!"

Six

Meg stood still, her hand tightened on a latch that was no
longer there. She had forgotten about Kenny.

There was a moment's quiet.

Then steps began, crunching on the pebbles
by the front porch. "Wilson? I said, *watch out.*
I'm coming in."

There was now the sound of boots on gritty
wood.

Kenny was inside the house!

A moment later, Meg heard a crash, a high-pitched squeal, then a scuffle. Good old E.T., she thought. With any luck, he's gone clear through the floor.

She ran out into the open, followed by Sue. Which way? Which way? "Well, lead on!" she snapped. "You're supposed to be the expert."

Sue wavered back and forth, her hands stretched out in front of her, as though she were playing Blind Man's Bluff.

"Meg—the path—it's gone!"

"What do you mean, *gone!*" Paths didn't just *go!*

The crashing came nearer. Kenny or Rip kicked Meg's gasoline can.

"I swear," Sue went on, "it was right here. And it took me straight to Dr. Greaves's back fence."

More crashing. Kenny was at the back door.

"Path or no path, let's get out of here. I'll lead. If we don't find your precious fence, we'll surely find another."

Meg plunged in, sweeping aside bushes smothered in wild vine until she ran smack into a tree.

"Bother, Sue! You got us into this!"

"Heehaw!" Kenny yelled. "I hear you loud and

clear, Wilson. And I know where you're headed. You'll not make it now!"

Meg ran, half sobbing, branches tearing her costume, her hands, her face. Her only wish was to find a way out. Here, or here, or here, must be Sue's fence. She'd reach it any minute now, and when she did, she would throw pride to the winds, climb up it, and scream and scream and scream . . .

A sudden woodchuck hole sent her sprawling and brought Sue down on top of her.

"Ow! Get off! You clumsy oaf!"

Meg struggled up, brushing dirt and leaves off her cloak and the legs of her jeans underneath. Then she became conscious of the silence. . . . No owl. No wind. No Kenny. No E.T.

She also became conscious of something else: There was no Dr. Greaves's fence, either. "What now, cleverclogs?" she whispered uneasily.

But Sue was not listening. Instead, she was standing, staring up through the trees. Clouds, scudding across the cold sky, had moved on to reveal a round white moon overhead.

"Look." Sue pointed. "Oh, Meg, look."

Meg looked.

"So what?" She picked at the sticky burrs that were clinging to her legwarmers. "What I want to know is, where is that fence? And where is

44

Kenny Stover? Oh, gosh, Sue, you don't think he's gone on ahead?"

Sue did not answer. "I'm scared," she said, as if to herself.

"Now what's there to be afraid of in an old moon, eh? You know, Sue, sometimes you really are *weird.*"

Sue shook her head. "You don't understand," she said. "This morning before school, I looked in the almanac to see how bright it would be for the school party tonight."

"So?"

"I thought what a shame it was. According to the table, the moon is in *conjunction.*"

"Speak English."

"That means that the moon is the exact opposite of full. In other words—don't you see, Meg? Tonight, in our world . . . there is no moon!"

Seven

"What do you mean, 'in our world'? What are you talking about?"

"I mean that wherever we are, it's not off Horse Hollow Road."

"Don't be silly. Where else could we be? Of course it is. We're somewhere in the lot behind Millford Drive."

"And it's Halloween," finished Sue in a low voice.

"Why, the girl's gone bonkers!"

"All right, Meg." Sue put her hands on her hips. "Explain Mother Baldry, and the cottage suddenly becoming all bright and new."

"I already did, and if you don't like my idea, you'll have to come up with something better."

"I think," Sue said slowly, "that this place is haunted, and that Mother Baldry is a ghost."

Meg laughed, a small tight sound. "You call that 'better'? I call it a load of old cobbles! You said a minute ago that she was real—*and* her stew, too. And as a matter of fact, it's quite given me the bellyache with all this running around on top of it. Try again."

"Okay," Sue said. "I will, because neither of us has explained why we couldn't find Dr. Greaves's back fence."

"But I can," Meg said. "How about: we've been running in circles? It could be that simple."

Again, Sue was not listening. Instead, she said, "Meg, do you remember last year in England on T.V., that serial where those kids kept walking into the middle of a field and disappearing? What was it called? Time—Time—Time—"

"Timewarp," Meg said. "Forget it. This isn't the middle of a field."

"Oh, you're being deliberately dense. It was called Time*slip*; I remember now. They found a place where there was a hole in the barrrier between this time and the other times—or was it other *worlds*? Now, suppose that's what we've done, that we've gone through it. The question is, how do we get back again?"

"Easily. By the same way that we came." Meg looked about, trying to decide which way that had been.

"But what about Kenny?"

"Kenny?" Meg stood stiffly. "If he has any sense, he's gone home long ago. Which is where we should be by now. Come on, I don't know what Mother will say."

"But which way?" Sue called.

Meg was already off, into the trees.

"I don't like it." Sue stopped.

Over their heads, in a high, fierce wind, cloud ribbons streaked across the moon.

"Keep going," Meg called over her shoulder, feeling her way in the sudden dark.

"I'm trying, I'm trying," Sue said.

Suddenly, Meg's hand felt an emptiness on all sides. A moment later, she was tripped by a humongous tree root. She scrambled up, drawing back her foot to kick it in revenge.

Just then, the bedraggled cloud floated clear,

and in the bright moonlight, Meg squawked. It was just as well that she had not kicked the root for the root was a leg, a long human leg, and on the other end of it was the rest of Kenny Stover. He was sitting up against a big rock with his brother, Rip, lying fast asleep across his knees!

"Well, well, well! This is getting like Old Home Week. I take it you guys can't get out either?"

Meg halted in midflight. "What—are you doing down there?"

"Rip banged his head, and did in his ankle pretty bad. He's gone to sleep—and so have my legs."

Meg stared down.

"We thought you'd gone long ago," she said at last.

"Ditto. I wish we'd never come in here," said Kenny.

"Ditto-ditto," Meg said. "It's not that we haven't tried to get out."

"It's like—" Kenny said. "It's like we're not supposed to."

"Stop it! Stop it, both of you! You're frightening me!"

Kenny looked Sue up and down. "What's with her?"

Meg shrugged. "Ask her. Tell him, Sue. About

the moon, and Mother Baldry, and your stupid time hole.''

Sue looked sulky. "You tell him."

And so Meg did. When she had done, Kenny was looking disgusted. "I never heard such a lot of hooey in my life," he said. "How come I never saw that old woman and all?"

Meg's eyes flashed. "And *how come* you never found the fence, or the cottage again, or *any way out?*"

"Hey—Wilson—you're forgetting yourself. You just watch your mouth."

"And you watch yours, Kenny Stover. You're a slob!"

"And you're a snob!" His voice rose, threatening. "Boy, if this kid wasn't on my knee . . ." He leaned back again. "No wonder they all say you've got your nose in the air! Think yourself too good for regular guys. Teacher's pet. Getting out of school while everybody else's still working their brains out. And all to scrape a stupid fiddle. You tell me, what's that good for?"

Meg drew herself up. "Do you know what you are, Kenny Stover, besides mean and a slob? You're *prejudiced,* that's what. *And* you're dumb. So dumb you can't stand anybody else getting on!"

"I am not *so* dumb! I don't go for all that

school stuff, is all. And everybody knows it, except you. Nobody else calls me *dumb*. Next time your mom goes to get her car fixed, just try telling the guy that's fixing it that he's dumb and see where that gets you, because that's what I'm gonna be. Tell you what, Wilson, why don't you go back where you came from? You don't belong here. You don't like nobody, and nobody likes you. And you know what they say? They say you don't even like yourself!"

"Oh, really?" Meg felt herself beginning to shake with rage and hate and injured pride. "Well, just let me tell you—"

"Wait." Sue broke in. "This is getting us nowhere. Don't either of you want to go home?"

Meg looked at her in amazement.

Kenny grinned lazily up at Sue. "Hi, limey number two. They say you're the brainy one. Say," he looked from one to the other, "are you *really* sisters?"

Meg glared at him. "So what if we are?"

"She's much nicer'n you, Wilson, that's what. Anyway"—Kenny slipped out from under Rip, then stooped down to scoop him up—"since we're all going the same way, we might as well go together."

Meg opened her mouth on a smart reply, then closed it again.

"Hey," Kenny said as they all turned to go, "get the mask."

Sue bent to retrieve the E.T. mask. Meg stared up at Kenny standing tall in the bright moonlight. "Why?"

"Why, what?"

"Why did you chase me like that? What were you going to do to me?"

"What do you think, you jerk? Dunk you in the apple barrel. Pay you back for making me look a total idiot out there."

"That was no more than you did to me—and have been doing since I came to that school."

"Well, you shouldn't be such a snob, talking so stuck up—and always on about that weird witch-what's-'er-name." He stopped, looking from Meg to Sue and back again. "Hey," he went on, "if you're so keen on her as you make out, how come *she's* in that getup, and you're Red Riding Hood?"

Meg's mouth curled in contempt. "Real witches don't dress like that," she said. "Morgan le Fay was beautiful, and a queen. Why, she was so beautiful that even Merlin fell for her. She shut him up in a tree to get rid of him— which is what I wish I could do with you."

"Please," Sue said. "Don't start again. Come on, I'll lead the way."

"You do that," Kenny said, hitching Rip up higher in his arms. "And take her with you. She's a dog."

"And you're an ape," Meg snapped back.

They all moved off into the wood.

"I don't like this," Kenny called from behind. When nobody answered him, he went on, "I mean, we seem to have been going forever. Hey, slow down. I don't like the way this kid's sleeping, either." A moment later, he called, "Hey—look!" He pointed to a gray blur just ahead. "That looks like Rip's mask!"

"It is, that's why," Meg told him. "It's where I made Sue drop it the last time we passed by here. And that is the selfsame rock you were leaning against when we found you, Kenny Stover. We've passed it now at least six times."

Kenny bent and put Rip down. "Why didn't you say so sooner?"

"I wasn't sure until we dropped the mask last time around."

"Um." Kenny didn't sound impressed. "That's an old trick."

"And it worked."

Kenny flopped down beside Rip, his back against the rock. "I'm tired of lugging that kid around. I'm gonna take a break."

"No." Sue sounded nervous. "We ought to carry on."

"*You* carry on," Meg said. "We'll catch up with you the next time around." She sat, too, as far from Kenny as possible.

After a moment's indecision, Sue followed suit, but she was soon up again pacing restlessly. Meg grew sick of watching her, closed her eyes, and relaxed. Now that they had stopped, she became conscious of the cold again: in the air, coming up through the ground. She huddled deeper inside her cloak and hood, shivering.

"Oh, my goodness."

"Now what?" Meg opened her eyes irritably.

"Here." Sue sounded urgent. "Here. On the other side of the rock. Quick!"

With a pointed sigh, Meg stood up. "This had better be good," she said.

Eight

What were they looking at? Meg could not be sure. Some way off among the trees, tiny lights danced like fireflies. Fireflies—in late October?

"What's happing behind there?" Kenny stood up.

"Nothing," Meg said.

With a great show of nonchalance, Kenny edged up and peered around over her shoulder. Behind him, Rip stirred.

"Oh, wow!" Kenny moved out from the rock

to get a better view. The lights winked out.

"Now look what you've done!" Meg cried.

Rip got to his feet, his eyes wide and dark with sleep.

"Where are we, Kenny?" he whimpered. "Take me home, Ken. I wanna go home."

Meg eyed him with distaste. "So do we, ducky," she said.

"Leave the kid alone, Wilson," Kenny said. He stared into the dark. "Oh, boy, I'd give anything to get out of here."

As if in answer, the lights reappeared, right in front of them.

"Oh, my," Sue said, pressing her back up against the rock.

The lights danced nearer, swirling up into a tight column. Suddenly, the column condensed, and then split into four separate masses. Bit by bit, the masses formed definite shapes.

"Peter Pan," Meg murmured.

"Puck," said Sue.

"We got *four* E.T.'s!" Rip shouted, pulling excitedly on Kenny's sleeve.

The spidery creatures capered around them.

"Who are you? *What* are you?" Meg cried.

In reply, there came a hissing and a spitting that sounded like an old toaster shorting out.

"I do believe," said Meg at last, "they are trying to look like us."

"How do you know?" Kenny sounded scornful. "They don't look like us one bit."

"I said, *trying.* And I don't know how I know. I just do; that's all. They are . . ." She stopped talking, waiting for the idea to finish forming in her head. ". . . points of energy and . . . they can't *see* us in the regular way. They are taking our shapes from ideas we have of ourselves in our minds." Meg looked surprised at herself.

"Not in *my* mind," Kenny said. "In *your* mind. That's why they look so weird." Without warning, he reached forward and touched one. His hands passed right through it, scattering it into random sparks again, but the sparks re-formed immediately into shapes.

Kenny laughed with delight. "How about that! It prickled! Like the pins and needles I got in my legs!" He rubbed his hands together briskly.

The figures took on finer resolution now, with long, thin faces and bony arms and legs.

"I was right." Kenny laughed. "They really look like you now, Wilson!"

Meg ignored him. "What do you want?" she asked them.

Again the hissing and spitting. This time, one of them darted to the edge of the clearing and pointed off to the left. Then it came back, reached out, and lifted the sleeve of Meg's cape.

Kenny whistled. "What do you know. One

minute my hand goes right through it, then the next it grabs ahold of you like it was a solid one of us!"

Meg felt the gentle tug on her sleeve.

"You want me to follow you?

"You *don't* want me to follow you. What, then?"

It tugged and twittered again. Meg looked at Kenny and Sue.

"They want our costumes!" she cried. "The very idea!"

She turned back to the shapes. "You shan't have them. Buzz off!"

At these words, all four of the things came back together. They swirled up and up into a tall pillar of light, faster and faster, brighter and brighter. Their sound became more and more high-pitched until suddenly the pillar shape dissolved and re-formed into a shimmering outline of, what?

"It's the cottage!" cried Sue. "It—*they* are offering to show us the way out of here!'"

As she spoke, the lines broke, the sparks scattered, then re-formed into the four original figures.

This time, one of them took hold of E.T.'s robe and tugged.

Rip screamed. "Get away! Kenny, get this wispity thing off me!"

Kenny flapped his hands through the sparks.

"Get off, get off with you!" He turned to Meg. "*You* tell them. Say they can have all this stuff, but they have to show us out of here first."

Before she could oblige, the dancing shapes dissolved back into separate sparks and began to fade back into the trees.

"Oh, no! Now we'll never get home!" Sue ripped off her pointy hat and waved it wildly. "Come back! Come back! Here!"

In a trice, the sparks were back, and re-formed, dancing about in front of them.

"Don't," Meg warned her. "Listen, you are supposed to be the sensible one. Don't trust them."

"But we have to if we want to get out of here."

"It's a trick. They mean mischief," Meg insisted, adding as Sue handed over Mother's favorite shawl, "Don't say I didn't warn you."

"I wonder why they want this stuff," Kenny said. "I mean, it's not exactly as though they need it."

"I already told you: they want to hurt us," Meg said.

"Oh, come on. How do *you* know? Don't be such a party pooper, Wilson. Come on, give and let's get out of here."

Kenny stripped off his vampire's cloak and flapped it out in front of him at arm's length.

One of the creatures snatched it deftly, shrugged into it, and did a little jig. It looked so odd in the black cloak, with its sparkly head and hands and feet all wiggling up and down, that even Rip forgot his fear and laughed out loud.

Sue handed over the rest of her costume: the warm black skirt and cardigan.

"Now you, kiddo," Kenny said. Rip pulled his E.T. gown up over his head, exposing a thin, red-and-white striped sweater and jeans with a hole in the knee.

"That all you got on under there? Mom'll kill you when you get home."

Kenny took off his green down vest, leaving himself with a hooded Islanders' jacket. The vest reached right to Rip's knees.

Still the sparks hovered, waiting.

Reluctantly, Meg took off her cloak and held it out.

She shuddered in the bitter cold, and felt the whole layer of warmth that had lain under her costume fairly streaming out into space.

"Now"— Meg's voice was grim—"it's your turn. You have to lead us out."

For answer, the creatures jigged up and down, away into the trees, too fast to be followed.

"Hey!" Kenny cried. "Hey, you guys! Not so fast!"

But they were gone.

"Well," Meg said. "I hope you're all satisfied."

"You shut up, Wilson!" Kenny was angry. "Anybody can make a mistake."

"And some better than others. *She's* just given away Mother's best shawl."

Rip piped up. "Kenny, I wanna go home. Take me home."

Kenny quieted down at once.

"Hey, kiddo, don't get upset. It's only a game. Here, get over here." He crouched against the rock and pulled Rip into the crook of his arm. "That's it. Now, keep in close to me, and that'll keep you warm."

Rip wailed. "My leg hurts."

"Crybaby," Meg said under her breath. She huddled down also against the rock, as far as possible from Kenny without actually getting out of sight.

"Meg . . ."

"Be quiet, Sue."

"I don't like this place. You know what? I think something bad's just about to happen."

"Don't be daft. I said you've been watching too much T.V.," said Meg. Even so, Meg was beginning to feel more uneasy herself. Had it suddenly grown colder than ever? It must have.

Even her teeth were chattering, and not just on account of her lost costume.

"Funny," Kenny whispered. "Rip's gone off again, like he's been bopped on the head. Poor little sucker. His leg's swelled up something awful."

"We should bind it," Sue said.

"What with?"

"Well, Meg's got her leg warmers."

"Oh, no you don't." Meg wrapped her arms protectively around her knees. "If you're so keen on being a good Samaritan, you just give something of your own!"

"Well, and aren't you the—" Kenny began.

"Hush," said Sue. "Listen."

As soon as Meg took her mind off Kenny Stover, she heard it—the noise that Sue must have heard—a faint scritch-scratch in the bushes to their right.

"It's prob'ly nothing but an old racoon," Kenny said loudly.

"Then go and chase it off," Meg said, shrinking more closely against the rock.

Ken got up, swaggered to the edge of the darkness, and peered out. The noise stopped. Kenny turned back toward them.

"There. What'd I say!"

"Look out!" Sue screamed.

Nine

Meg was not at all sure what exactly happened, only that something big burst out of the trees, sent Kenny sprawling, leapt over him, and made for the rock. Sue screamed again, and ran off into the trees.

Fast as she could, Meg scrambled up and followed blindly after. When at last they slowed down, Sue was crying.

"Oh, stop sniveling." Meg was bent nearly double, her hands braced on her knees, waiting for the pain in her ribs to subside.

"But Meg, Meg . . ."

"Shut up."

"What about Kenny and—"

"I said, *shut up,* and if you don't, I'll—I'll go off without you, so there!" How, how—*how* were they going to get home? She straightened up. She wished Sue would stop blubbing. She almost handed over her clean hanky, but quickly changed her mind. "Stop it. Come on, let's go."

"But, Meg—"

"Do you, or don't you want to get out of here?"

"I do, but—"

"Move!"

Sue moved, close at Meg's heels.

What Meg disliked most about the place was the quiet. She recalled hearing the owl in the ruined cottage. Then it had startled her, but she wished she could hear it now. She thought about the Mexican pottery owls that Mother had begun to collect on the mantelshelf, about the macrame owl plant holder hanging beside the kitchen sink, about the owl that Sue had brought home from school two weeks before, and of the fun she had made of it. (An *owl?* It looks more like something you dug up out of the back-yard!) She thought of owls, of hot cocoa, and tomorrow's test in social studies—of anything and everything but what had happened and those whom they had left behind. She pushed away the memory of Kenny falling, and of the big thing leaping over him toward Rip, who'd been lying there, fast asleep.

She stumbled, nearly fell. The ground had been dropping down quite steeply all around them into a deep hollow. Damp mist was on her skin, and in her throat. There was an earthy smell of soggy leaves and toadstools. Meg did not like that cold and that clinging damp.

She wanted to stop and climb back the way they had come, but she lacked the will to turn. Anyway, she told herself, they had come down so far. What went down was bound to turn up again in the end, so it might be quicker just to go on.

Down they went, down into a deeper quiet and darkness: there was not much moonlight under that canopy of dead vine and matted trees.

"Sue?"

"Here." Sue's voice was hoarse.

"This isn't like any place we've ever been. I'm scared."

"Me, too. And I can't see you at all."

65

Meg reached back for Sue's hand.

"I'll lead now, if you like," Sue said.

"No. Tell you what: we'll go together."

It was clumsy, and slow, but Meg felt better traveling that way. At least if anything came at them now it would be more likely to grab them both at once.

Down, down, and still down, around gnarled tree trunks and over rotten logs they went. Dead blackberry canes snagged their jeans, their sleeves, their hair.

Meg's mind began to wander; her feet slowed. She fought an urge simply to sit down and give up.

They came to an abrupt stop on the edge of a clearing and stared out dumbly at what they saw: in the middle of that space stood a solitary stone slab lit by a single shaft of moonlight; a waist-high, black rectangular slab that seemed to suck the moonbeam down into its very depths.

Under that stone's spell, Meg crept out into the open, Sue at her heels. They both sat cross-legged, staring at it.

Meg's eyes gradually closed.

The everyday world seemed so unreal now. So far away. So . . . unimportant.

Images came into her mind: of a white face,

a beautiful face, with great dark eyes, bright red lips, and black hair piled high, crowned with a jet black diadem; of a long body wreathed in fine dark stuff that floated about it like mist on the surface of a cold lake. Meg knew that face, knew it well, for had she not dreamed and day-dreamed about it these past years? It was her very own face as it had been many lifetimes before, or so she liked to imagine: the face of Morgan le Fay with its all-knowing smile—powerful and cool . . .

Her thoughts stirred as though something had ruffled their surface. Morgan le Fay would not be traipsing around lost within yards of her own back door. Neither would she make a sitting target of herself in such a sinister place as this.

"Meg . . ." Sue's voice sounded as though it were coming through a wall. "I am having such a bad dream, like the ones I used to have when I was young. You know . . ." Sue's voice faded away, and Meg almost forgot her, until she went on, ". . . that one where I am running from these people and I can't move and they are getting closer and closer . . . and closer. . . ." Sue started to cry softly.

Meg pushed herself up from the ground and took Sue's hand. "We must," she began, and then forgot what they must.

Move, a voice inside her urged. *Move. Away. Go on. Morgan le Fay would not let herself be so beguiled. With a few magic words she would be out of this place . . .*

Meg, coming awake, recalled her fear by the broken-down fence on far off Horse Hollow Road. And not only did she recall it, but she also recognized now that its source was here in this place, powerful and undiluted.

And the name of this source, this essence? It was *Evil.* That clearing—no, that *stone* was evil: and *Evil* was that stone.

We must get out of here, she thought with sudden urgency.

With a great effort she pulled Sue up into a walk, feeling as though she were now sharing Sue's nightmare—or wading like a diver along the deep sea floor.

She had a growing sense that something very, very dangerous was advancing toward them at great speed.

"Sue, let's go. Go, go—*go!*"

Somehow, Meg dragged Sue out of the clearing, then on, and on . . . and on.

After a time, Meg let go of Sue's hand. She felt her terrible panic fading, felt it being left behind. A strong conviction grew upon her then that they had been in peril of their lives.

"Who knows what might have happened if we'd stayed by that awful stone," she muttered to herself.

"What?"

"Nothing. I say" —Meg raised her voice—"I think we are going up again. Yes, we are."

"Hooray," Sue cried. "You know, I began to feel quite funny down in that hollow, didn't you?"

Meg, more herself by the minute, didn't bother to reply. Her leg warmers and her jeans were soaked through, and her toes were squelching in her socks.

"I don't care what happens," she declared aloud a few minutes later. "Nobody—but *nobody* will ever get me to go down there again!"

Ten

They crested the rise and went on until the trees thinned out into a wide clearing quite different from the one down in the hollow. Here were silvered grass and dappled spaces and shining clumps of birch. Yet there was still that unearthly hush, even here. No owl, no racoon, not even the stir of a leaf broke the silence.

Meg led the way out from under the murky trees.

"This is better." She looked back over her shoulder at Sue. "I thought we'd never get out of there." She took a deep breath of relief—and held it, following Sue's startled glance. There, in front of them, hovered a cluster of pale figures.

It was too late to pull back.

The cluster closed up, until, after a moment, one of the figures left it to walk over toward them.

"Oh, my," Meg whispered. And, "Wow."

The woman was beautiful—almost as beautiful as Meg imagined Morgan le Fay to have been.

"Welcome. I am so glad you have come to us at last."

A lump came into Meg's throat at the sound of the woman's voice. It was warm, human, and very, very English. Had she and Sue been expected?

"Are you from Home—from England?"

The woman shook her head. "No. Nor from any place in your world. I am neither what you see, nor what you hear. Wherever you came from, I would speak in your tongue."

"Oh," Meg said. She looked around. "Who are

you? Where are we, and . . . do you know the way out?"

The woman smiled, and made a slight bow.

"I am Greylen of the Birchen Tree, and these are my friends."

"Oh, Meg." Sue was overawed. "They aren't, I bet. She's a queen, and they're her subjects."

Meg glared at Sue. Trust her to state the obvious! Why, anyone with half an eye could see that. The heads of the six women with Greylen were wreathed in berries and thorn, but Greylen wore a crown, a silver crown, studded with tiny points of light that winked under the moon. All of them, Greylen and her women, wore simple shifts down to their ankles, of a shadowy stuff that shimmered like gossamer wet with rain. Their shoulders and arms and feet were quite bare. Meg shivered.

"As for where you are . . . you are in the Wood this night."

"I already know that," Meg answered her impatiently. "But which one?"

"Just, the Wood. It is any and every wood that has been or ever will be. Save for one difference." Her smile faded, leaving her face haunted and sad.

72

Meg was not interested. "Can you get us out of here?"

"Oh, yes. Your third question. The one that I feared you would ask."

Feared? Meg caught the word. "You can't help us, then?"

"It is not that." The queen regarded her solemnly. "I had rather hoped your question would be a different one."

"Speak English."

"Meg!"

"Very well," Greylen said. "Four of you came in here this night. Is it truly your wish that only two of you leave?"

Meg bristled. "The other two are no concern of mine. I didn't ask them to chase us in."

"Meg!"

"Anyway, we've had enough of this place. So—can you help us out, or no?"

Greylen studied her for a moment. "Please wait here," she said at last.

She turned and walked away from them, taking four of the six women with her. The other two stayed behind to watch Meg and Sue.

Meg turned her back on them and on Sue as well. Why should she feel so bad about Kenny and Rip? They weren't really her affair, were they? It was Kenny's fault that they were all in there. It was his fault that they were lost. Whatever happened to Kenny and Rip from now on was no business of hers.

She thought of his awful manners, of the names he called her, of the way he mocked her accent and Morgan le Fay and her violin. And, worst of all, of the way he had dismissed her that very night:

Tell you what, Wilson, why don't you go back where you came from? You don't belong. You don't like nobody, and nobody likes you . . .

But other thoughts overrode those: of him sitting against the big rock with E.T. sleeping across his knees, of him walking so long carrying Rip in his arms, of him giving Rip his own down waistcoat, of him striding out to chase off a racoon . . .

"No!" she cried, pushing that image away.

"Meg?"

She kept her head averted.

"I don't know what Mother is going to say," Sue whispered at last.

Mother? Meg's troubled feelings finally found an outlet.

An old familiar anger welled inside her: at Mother, at Sue, at Kenny and the whole world. It was all their fault that she was stuck here, and when she tried to leave, she was treated like a monster. What was that Greylen doing, anyway?

"She has gone to consult the Three Sisters."

Meg spun around, horrified. Why, those two women had read her thoughts!

"Thoughts, words, intentions, deeds—they are all the same to us, Meg-Wilson. Wishes, feelings, desires . . . all these we receive in here, and here." The speaker touched her brow and her heart.

Meg-Wilson! They even knew her name, even though they did say it as though it were one word. The busybodies. The prying, peeking busybodies, poking around in her private thoughts—and not offering to raise a finger to help! Why, she'd tell Greylen. She'd give the Birch Queen a piece of her mind. Right now this minute, just let them all see if she wouldn't!

She strode away from them along the route that Greylen had taken, ignoring Sue's calls for her to come back.

On she went, her head high, knowing what she was going to do, knowing that she was certain to regret it afterwards. Meg was not a little frightened at herself, yet unable for all that to pull back before it was too late.

Nobody tried to stop her.

The clearing stretched back to the foot of a steep incline, a cliff, really. At the foot of the cliff was the mouth of a small cave, and clustered around that cave mouth were the four women who had gone with Greylen, looking in.

Meg kept going. Driven by her anger, she shoved past them into the cave.

Eleven

Around the center of the floor squatted three women, their heads shrouded in more of the cobwebby stuff. They were gazing at a round, flat stone in the middle of the circle, a stone of about coffee table height, a white stone that glowed like moonlight. From it came the strangest sound, a kind of thin whining hum, like wind in a high sooty chimney.

The sight of it reminded Meg of another stone, the black slab down in the cold, dark place. She pictured them side by side—the oblong black stone that swallowed light, the round white stone that gave it off. The one was evil; the other, she sensed, was good.

What was the purpose of the stones? she wondered, never doubting that each had one.

She stared at the white stone, her anger forgotten.

Greylen was standing between the cave mouth and the circle of women. At Meg's entrance, she turned and nodded gravely.

Why, Meg realized, the queen had been waiting for her, had known that she would follow. She had half a mind to turn around and walk right out of there, but just then, Sue stepped in behind her. Anyway, she was curious to see what happened next.

Greylen spoke, this time without even opening her mouth. Into Meg's mind, the words came clearly:

Sisters, behold Meg-Wilson and Sue of the Outer World.

The Three Sisters turned their heads and nodded.

Oh, but how *ancient* they were, Meg saw, especially their eyes. But they were still beautiful, in their way, with round cheeks and high foreheads and kindly mouths. She found herself bobbing stiffly at the knee, nothing like the full curtsy to the ground that she'd seen ladies make to the queen on T.V. at Home in England.

You will please not speak, Greylen warned her. *The Three Sisters are locked into the Stone and any untoward noise will break the link. If you would ask me something, do it by thought alone.*

But I already have, Meg thought to herself, her resentment returning. I asked you plainly if you could get us out of here, and you have not answered me. Instead, here I am standing in this rotten little cave with three old women and a stupid old stone and lot of crazy mumbo jumbo about some kind of link that I can't see.

Then she remembered how everybody could read her mind, and she was mortified.

But if the queen had heard her, she gave no sign. Greylen was too busy gazing with the Sisters at the Stone. What were they all doing with it, anyway?

Even as she wondered, the whining sound grew louder and higher, round and round like a spiral stair, until it whirred painfully in her ears. Sue tried to take her hand, but Meg shook it off and moved away.

The noise stopped, and the air above the Stone shimmered. When the shimmering faded, there, above it, was the little clearing with the big rock where she and Sue had abandoned Kenny and Rip to the massive creature from the woods.

She stepped back toward Sue.

There they all were, just as they were in the flesh, only smaller: Sue standing about, and Meg with Kenny and Rip huddled against the rock.

Don't be scared, Meg told herself. It's a clever trick, but no more scary than the holograph you saw with Father at the trade fair last year, or the one of Princess Leia that R2-D2 carried around inside him in *Star Wars* . . .

Meg watched the holograph Sue move around, exactly as she had done earlier, Meg was sure, even though Meg was now looking at it all from the front. The real life Sue reached again for Meg's hand, and this time Meg let it stay.

The holograph Sue stopped dithering and spoke. Meg, typically, recalled the words exactly:

Meg . . .

She mouthed her own reply with the holograph Meg.

Be quiet, Sue.

I don't like this place. You know what? I think something bad's just about to happen.

Don't be daft. I said you've been watching too much T.V.

The real life Sue squeezed her hand.

She saw Kenny looking down at Rip. Hadn't he said something about Rip having gone off to sleep—*like he's been bopped on the head,* or something like that?

She closed her eyes. This was a dream. A bad dream. And she was home in bed at 32a Millford Drive, Locust Valley, Long Island, New York, U.S.A. . . .

When she opened her eyes again, Kenny was up on his feet, sauntering to the edge of the bushes.

Oh, no . . .

It's prob'ly nothing but an old racoon, he'd said. She tried to turn away, but could not. This was the part of the movie where she'd usually go out to the bathroom—but this was no movie.

Kenny reached the edge of the clearing and turned back. From her new vantage point in front of the rock she now saw only the back of his head, but she remembered well enough the cocky grin on his face, and his words: *There. What'd I say?*

Behind Meg, Sue took in a short, sharp breath. A monstrous shadow, a horned, two-legged creature bounded out of the bushes and knocked

Kenny down——No! It didn't knock him down at all, but only touched him lightly with some sort of stick, which it then put back in its . . . pouch? It was too dark to see. Anyway, having downed Kenny, it leapt over him and moved toward the rock where Rip slept and the holograph Meg cowered. Meg watched the holograph Sue's mouth open in a scream, watched Sue run, watched herself follow. How fast they had taken off . . .

Enough! she cried, toward Greylen, but still the images continued.

The creature, without having given her or Sue a second glance, stooped down and lifted Rip as though he were no more than a rag doll—which is what he looked like, dangling in the creature's great arms.

It wasn't after us at all, was it? Meg asked Greylen. *It wanted Rip all the time. Why? Why did it want him? Where has it taken him?*

Still Greylen did not answer her, or even move. It was as though she had not heard Meg's thought at all. The creature stepped over Kenny to go back the way he had come.

Meg saw then that the horn was not a horn but a spike on a steely helmet that glinted in the moonlight.

Why, the creature was a *man*—a soldier. He

was in full regalia, including cloak and boots and the strange stick that Meg had already nick-named the *dreamstick*. Meg could see clearly now that he had stuffed it into his uniform belt.

He advanced forward out of the clearing, straight toward Meg. She tensed, ready to run, but she need not have worried. As soon as he reached the ring of the Three Sisters, he van-ished, as did the clearing, leaving Meg in the dark still holding Sue's hand.

She broke free and ran from the cave.

Meg-Wilson—wait! Greylen stood in the cave mouth.

Meg thrust out her lower lip. "I want to go." She said it aloud deliberately.

First you must see three visions. So say the Three Sisters. Of what is past, of what is now, and of what is to come.

Why? The question was sullen.

Greylen shrugged gracefully. *That is not for me to say.*

But I bet you know all the same, Meg thought. She followed the queen back inside.

The air above the Stone was shimmering again.

Another vision, Meg thought. They are going to show me something else. When the shim-mering cleared, she saw a vast cavern in miniature, so vast that she could not see its roof. How odd, she thought, to see such a huge, high cavern fitted inside this little, low cave!

At the far end of the high cavern was a flight of steps. At the top of those steps stood a throne. Behind the throne, the wall glowed an unearthly purple, like the inside of the game arcade in the mall at Roosevelt Field.

Meg began to feel a cold, the same cold she had felt by the broken fence in front of the ruined cottage on Horse Hollow Road and again by the black slab down in the dark hollow.

Something moved so suddenly that she jumped backward onto Sue's toes. Things—creatures—slithered from the shelter of the cavern walls out onto the floor. Earthen creatures, Meg thought, made of lumps of leaf mold and rot and mildew and old sacks. Ragged masks hid their faces, and their bare gray limbs oozed over the stones like leeches. They looked so real, and so close, that it was hard to believe that they could not just reach out and touch her. She drew back.

Suddenly, a flight of great brown things, part human, part bird, leapt into the cavern on semi-useless wings. Their cloaks flew, flashing purple on the underside, the coxcombs atop their helmets flapping with the thrust of their leaps.

These Leapers went to stand by the throne as the floor filled with what looked to Meg like the second Halloween parade of the evening. There were men and women and boys and girls of all ages, *from* all Ages. Why, some of them looked as if they had stepped right out of her old coloring book, *Historical Costumes from Around the World*. There was a Roman senator in his toga and a matron from Hellenic Greece in her yellow chiton bordered with bright blue waves. There, a tall young Cossack, and beside him, a beautiful Spanish girl with red lace mantilla and fan. While over there, in ragged pants and frayed straw hat, looking just like an illustration from her beloved *Adventures of Huckleberry Finn*, was a young lad, his skin still burned from the summer sun, chewing on a corncob pipe.

In they came, spilling out of the passages into the cavern until it was crammed. No, Meg decided, they didn't look like people in a costume parade after all, but more like the dummies in Madame Tussaud's Waxworks Museum, neither alive nor dead.

There was a movement at the edge of the crowd. The creatures surged, then parted to let something pass slowly into view. Like the brown-and-purple Leapers, it was part bird, part human, but unlike them, it was more bird than man. It was almost as large as Meg herself—or would be, seen life-size, Heaven forbid. It had the beak of a vulture, a ragged crest of blue-black plumes, and bright red rings around its eyes. As it advanced, its bony pinions moved up and down, and Meg saw, to her horror, that at their tips were human hands like claws. Like one of the Harpies, she thought, those ghastly bird-women in the old Greek tales who used to carry off the souls of the dead . . .

When it reached the throne, it hopped up to perch on the left arm and began to preen itself with its beak and fingernails.

A wild wind riffled the heads of those gathered in that place, and Meg's skin crawled. *Stop!* she wanted to shout. *Stop!* But before she could, a swirl of silver and black streaked in, scattering everyone to the floor.

Meg put her hands to her face and bent over.

When she straightened up again, a figure was standing at the top of the steps, looking straight down the cavern and into her eyes.

Twelve

Meg stared, the words forming on her lips unconsciously:

Morgan le Fay . . .

It was her, wasn't it? Morgan le Fay, King Arthur's sister, the witch queen, as Meg had pictured her, and as she had seen her in that strange dream down in that terrible, dark hollow.

Meg drew her arms across her chest as if to protect herself.

Looking into that white face, she now saw something she had not noticed before. The mouth was cruel, the eyes were pitiless, and the whole face devoid of humanity. How could she have wanted to look like that!

She squeezed her eyes shut. A tear trickled down her cheek.

Greylen's voice came gently into her mind.

Behold not your Morgan le Fay, but Samana, Dark Queen, who has plagued our Wood these many Ages. By her throne sits her familiar, part human, part crow, and part raven: the Craven that feeds on the souls of those whom Samana would take to herself on All Hallows' Eve.

Meg continued to stare at this queen whom Greylen had called Samana. She can't really be looking at me, she can't, Meg told herself. She's only a 3–D projection that's somehow coming from that white stone.

But she was relieved when Samana turned her head away to look over the multitude.

When that multitude was still, Samana sat and clapped her hands three times. On anyone else they would have been lovely hands: white fingered, long, and expressive. But when she beckoned, they looked like talons.

In answer to Samana's signal, a pathway opened up through the crowd, leading to the foot of the throne. Along that pathway trod a massive figure with a spiked helmet atop its head. It was the soldier who'd sent Meg and Sue racing from the rock.

As he reached the foot of the dais steps, Samana gestured him to kneel. This he did with energy, scraping sparks off the stone floor with his spike.

Samana's mouth curled into a snarl. The soldier pointed back the way he had come. What was he saying? Meg, already guessing the answer, refused to let it pop into her mind.

The Dark Queen dismissed the soldier with a flick of her hand. What for? To do what? Meg shifted uneasily.

The soldier did not move. His broad back was outlined against the throne steps. Why did he not stand up? Was he too afraid? Or was he— surely not—defying Samana's commands. Again the Dark Queen waved him away, without result. Faint hope came into Meg's heart at the soldier's refusal, until Samana stood angrily and started down the steps toward him.

She was but two steps from the bottom when the soldier—the *Spike*, as Meg decided to call him—leapt up and out the way he had come, waved on by the crowd.

What had passed between them, the Spike and

the Dark Queen? Where was Kenny now? Was he still lying by the rock where they had left him? And—Meg swallowed—did Samana know about her and Sue? And if she did, would Samana send the Spike out for them too? Meg began to feel comforted by the little cave and Greylen and the Three Sisters and the round white stone.

Samana did not go back up to her throne again, but waited at the foot of the steps. The Craven hopped off its perch and fluttered down to crouch at her heel. It looked more like a Harpy than ever, Meg decided: a ravenous, filthy Harpy, waiting to feast on a lost soul.

That last thought really upset her. She shook the image off, but Greylen's words came back: . . . *the Craven that feeds on the souls of those whom Samana would take to herself on All Hallows' Eve.*

Meg's thoughts tumbled faster and faster. Words and images pounded the barrier that she had set against them.

The spiked helmet gleaming in the darkness . . . Kenny lying senseless on the ground . . . the cold dark hollow—far worse than that vast cavern pictured over the round white stone . . . the Craven with its cruel beak and hungry, red-ringed eyes . . .

And words, words, words . . .

First you must see three visions. . . . Of what is past, of what is now, and of what is to come. . . .

This was the second vision, wasn't it? Of what was happening right now. Somewhere, in this strange Wood, even as she was standing in this little cave with Greylen and the Three Sisters, so were all those creatures and Samana assembled in that horrid cavern waiting for—

As much as she didn't want to, Meg kept her eyes on the scene.

The Spike was back.

Behind him walked two ghastly creatures. Were they human? Meg could not tell. They wore stark white bird masks with stiff black crests, and towered head and shoulders above the rest of the crowd.

They advanced slowly in single file, and the reason for this became clear as they moved into full view. Between them they bore a litter, and on it lay a small figure dressed in a green down vest, a thin red-and-white striped sweater, and jeans with a hole in the knee. Like it or not, Rip was at that moment being carried to the foot of the Dark Queen's throne.

Thirteen

The two bearers laid down the litter at the foot of the steps, then backed off to stand on either side of it. Samana looked down. Behind her, the Craven edged closer, opening and closing its claws, working its pinions slowly up and down. Surely it was not going to—

Not yet, Meg-Wilson. On the stroke of mid-

night shall she take the little one, and in the Deepest, Darkest Part of the Wood. She is only looking him over now.

Samana bent further and laid a white hand on Rip's brow. The Craven, beside her, raised its head and opened its hooked beak wide. Although no sound came from the holograph, Meg put her hands to her ears.

Samana straightened triumphantly, raising her arms to acknowledge the homage of the crowd. Then, to Meg's horror, the Dark Queen pointed down at Rip and Rip stirred and sat up, rubbing his eyes. Meg watched him peering out into the dark. He's looking for Kenny, she thought. He's going to yell any minute for Kenny to take him home.

But the next moment Samana's arm cut the air above Rip's head, and he went down again like a stone. Amid the shouts of the multitude, the Dark Queen gestured the bearers to take Rip away. Then she stepped back up to gloat upon her throne. And as Samana looked out again, it seemed to Meg that the queen was looking straight at her. Their eyes locked, and Meg felt a queer pull, a sort of *drift* in her head. Me, Meg thought. Samana wants me, too.

Her knees went weak.

On the contrary, my dear, Greylen replied.

Whatever that means, thought Meg, but she could not respond, held as she was by Queen Samana's gaze. She felt herself growing smaller, weaker. I am nothing, she thought. I am a worthless speck. Samana could crush me by her look alone if she were truly here.

Just as she felt she would buckle under or pass out, the image faded, and Meg was freed from that terrible regard.

Why, she thought savagely, why are those three horrible old women and Greylen putting us through this? All we want is to get out of here. Too bad about Rip, but there is Kenny. He's Rip's brother. He's the one they should be talking to.

Almost without pause, the shimmering came again, fading out this time into near blackness. At its center was an area of total dark that Meg recognized at once.

It was the deep hollow, still empty save for the baleful stone. What had Greylen just called that place? *The Deepest, Darkest Part of the Wood*—the place to which Samana had just ordered the bearers to take Rip.

First you must see three visions. . . . Of what is past, of what is now, and of what is to come. . . .

Then this was the third vision, of what was

going to happen. But when? Why—at midnight, of course!

On the stroke of midnight shall she take the little one, Greylen had said.

Meg stared at the deserted hollow with dread. What was she doing here, wasting time, watching? Why didn't she just walk out and away? Because, she reminded herself in alarm, Greylen wouldn't help her and Sue until the Sisters had finished running their picture show.

A movement caught her eye.

Yes, over there, to the left in the holograph.

She grunted in disgust. They were distinct now, those crawly leechy things from the high cavern, oozing out from among the dark trees. And there! Just as she had expected them, the brown-and-purple Leapers came flying in through the branches, toward the black slab. But not too close, not too close.

Then many dark shapes emerged to crowd the edges, the poor lost people, the Halloween parade people with faces neither alive nor dead. All those folk Samana had taken over the years when her world had touched theirs on All Hallows' Eve. She remembered old Mother Baldry still waiting on her world's edge. Is that what had happened to her son? Was he now there among them and one of them?

There was a growing air of expectancy; she could feel it. Heads turned again and again to peer out into the shadows around the clearing.

Samana was coming. But which way? Which way?

Three new figures appeared now, ones Meg had not seen back in the cavern. They were tall—taller even than the litter bearers, and stick thin. They looked to Meg like the figures on Gran Jenkins's tarot cards—or like mummies. Their entire bodies were cocooned in gray, except for the circle of their faces. Through a slit in their gray cocoons their right fists protruded.

They are the Three Mummers, symbols of Death, Greylen explained. *You see the first one with the purple berries on its head? Now see what it carries in its right hand: that forked root is the root of the mandrake plant that some call mandragora, and those are mandrake berries on its head. That Mummer stands for forgetfulness.*

Now, see, Meg-Wilson: the second one passes by. See the vines on its head and the tangle of creepers in its hand? They are not really vines and creepers, but the limbs of the ceiba tree, the jungle tree that smothers ancient temples and monuments in your Far Eastern world. That Mummer represents entombment.

Now here comes the third.

Meg looked, and recognized for herself what that one stood for. The figure's head sprouted the fungus stinkhorn, which she had seen so often in her English woods. In its hand, it bore a short wooden wand half eaten by the same.

Decay, she told Greylen. *It stands for decay.*

Not so much decay, as transition from one state to another, Greylen answered.

Which surely amounted to the same thing, Meg thought, though it was a more positive way of putting it, she had to admit.

What have they come for? she asked.

There was a pause.

Well, as you have guessed, we are looking ahead, Greylen told her at last. *Soon this will all happen in the Deepest, Darkest Part of the Wood. At the stroke of midnight, those three will touch your friend—*

He is not my friend!

—and then will come Samana and touch him too. At that moment, he will become one of her multitude.

Meg said nothing. What was there to say?

Now came the Craven, moving its pinions up and down in its slow, deliberate way, clearing a path through the crowd all the way to the black slab. Meg fully expected the creature to hop up and perch beside Rip but instead, he squatted by the stone, careful not to touch it.

Now came the stirring in the trees. Why, Meg could almost feel the icy wind fanning her cheeks. But it was not Samana, not yet. It was the awful Spike, waving people aside with his dreamstick, and the two bearers, bringing Rip on the litter.

Through the dead-alive assembly they went until they reached the black slab. There, at the Spike's direction, the bearers raised the litter on high, then set it down gingerly atop the stone.

Meg bit her lip. How old was Rip? Six? He had to be for first grade. But he didn't look it, lying there on that vile stone that nobody would touch. She shuddered. Poor thing. For she realized now that the stone was really an altar, the altar upon which each member of that motley crowd had once lain, and that Rip was going to be Samana's latest sacrifice.

And soon.

The thought made Meg afraid.

In that instant, Samana whirled in, in a fury of impatience. The crowd fell back under the energy of her advance and a space rapidly cleared around the slab. She circled the stone, defining her territory, defying anyone to overstep its bounds.

As one, the mass began to sway—toward Rip, then away from him—like waves around a rock in a bay.

Samana signaled the Spike. He scuttled off somewhere, coming back at once with a twisted stick on which was mounted a yellowed skull.

That is the head of Goga, who was witch queen before Samana. Greylen's thought came sadly. *And so the evil goes on.*

Samana snatched the horrid scepter and raised it for all to see, and the mouths of the dead-alive folk opened in a silent shout. Then the Dark Queen wheeled around the space, tantalizing the outstretched hands with the skull, while beneath her the Three Mummers moved to the altar and waved their strange maces over Rip's head. First the Mandrake, then the Ceiba, then the Stinkhorn.

Faster the witch queen whirled, and faster, until, suddenly, she turned and ran up to the slab. Even she did not touch it, but, leaning over, she raised the skull on high.

"No!" Meg cried, at the top of her voice, whereupon the light cut out, the scene vanished, and all was dark in the little cave.

Fourteen

Meg was halfway across the clearing when Sue caught up with her. She stopped, secretly thankful. After all, where could she have gone? Back down into that dark hollow?

"Wherever are you going, Meg?"

"Where do you think? Home, of course. *They* obviously aren't going to help us." She rammed her hands into her jeans pockets. "Anyway," she added, "you can mind your own business. You don't understand."

"But I do," Sue said. "Every bit as much as you. I saw what you saw. And heard everything that Greylen told you. And I'm just as scared as you."

"I'm not scared in the least," Meg said.

"Greylen wants you to come back, Meg. She really is going to help us now. She promised."

"Don't you believe it." Meg glanced at the dark cave mouth where the Birch Queen stood waiting. Despite her words, Meg walked back toward her.

"This Wood is all trick and no treat!" she cried as soon as she was near enough. "First those wispy things cheat us out of our good warm clothes, and now you sell us a peep show with empty promises!"

"Ah, yes, your clothes," Greylen spoke aloud, smiling faintly. "I feared that that might happen when I asked them to help. Elementals are so irresponsible, and ever prone to mischief."

Elementals! Gran Jenkins had told Meg lots about them. They were spirits so primitive that they scarcely had any mind at all. And hadn't she herself somehow recognized at the time that that was what the wispy things were? "Points of energy," she'd called them. Yet mindless or no, they had managed to cheat four human children out of their Halloween costumes. And here was this Greylen admitting that she had set them up to it!

"Why?" Meg demanded. "Why didn't you come yourself to show us the way out if you were so concerned about us?"

"Because," Greylen answered her, "tonight is All Hallows' Eve. On this night, just as Samana is strong, so are we weak. Tonight we are confined to the safety of the clearing and the cave. See."

Greylen turned and went back into the little cave. When she came out again a moment later, she was carrying what looked like a young birch wand, slender and straight.

"Behold, Meg-Wilson!" Greylen raised the wand above her head, and at once it began to shine with a white light, brighter and brighter until Meg was forced to look away.

"This is my staff," Greylen said. "No power in this Wood may withstand it, not even Samana—save on All Hallows' Eve. Tonight, if I take but one step out of this place, this power will not prevail. See."

Greylen walked out to the first fringe of trees. She took one step beyond the clearing, then another, and another. Suddenly, there was a blue flash, and the light was gone, and Greylen was left holding what looked like an ordinary birch wand.

The instant Greylen reentered the clearing, the wand began to glow once more, but more dimly, as though the flash had spent some of its energy.

"You see, Meg-Wilson? I tell you truly: only here is my power intact tonight. Out there, it is void."

"Then you can't help us after all." Meg shot Sue a look that said, "told you so."

"We can help you to help yourselves—and one another."

Meg ignored Greylen's last words. "How—help ourselves?"

"The Sisters offer three tools for your use if you would win this night." Greylen set her staff aside and held out her hands. In her palms, three small objects glittered in the moonight.

She held up one of them. It was a crystal, about one inch long, and shaped like a rowboat.

"This," she said, "is a pathstone. You hold it loosely in your hand, like this"—she cupped her palm —"and think *hard* of where you want to go, or whom you want to see. The stone will twist around and point you in the right direction. But you must keep your thoughts firmly on your destination, or it will turn again and you will be led astray."

Greylen then held up the second object.

"This," she said, holding it up against the moon, "you must use to waken your two friends, for they have been touched by the dreamstick that Samana's lieutenant bears. Three drops on the tongue will do."

In the light the fluid glowed a rich ruby red.

"We won't need that, thanks, " Meg said. "Just the stone."

Greylen went on, "The third thing is this." She held up a tiny glass ball. It was colorless and about the size of a glass marble.

"It will serve you twofold. Hold it like so"— Greylen laid it in the cup of her palm—"and look into it with a firm will, and you will see what you need to see. Hold it like this"—she tightened her fist around the ball and held it high above her head—"and it will give you the power to stop Samana, just long enough to save the little one on the strike of midnight—but only if your will be strong."

Meg stared at the thing as though it were a hypodermic needle. "If they're all so powerful, why don't *you* use them!" she said.

"Meg!"

Greylen slowly shook her head. "Because as I have already explained, on this night I am weak. Only you have the power to use these tools, and that power is strong when one would save one's own kind."

"Take them, Meg," Sue said.

Meg turned on her. "*You* take them. You're the goody-goody around here. Here, Greylen— give them to her. She'll go charging off to the rescue at the drop of a hat."

"I only wish she could," Greylen said sadly. "She certainly has the courage, even if she doesn't think so now. And she has the brain. And also the will. But she hasn't the *power*."

Power?

"What sort of power? What do you mean?" Meg began to say, but stopped herself just in time. Greylen was leading her on again, trying to get her interested in spite of herself.

"Thank you," she said instead, "but if you'll give us the pathstone, we'll be on our way." She held out her hand.

Without a word, Greylen handed it over.

Meg bobbed. "I thank you. How will you get it back?"

"Oh, do not worry about that, Meg-Wilson. Nothing that belongs in this Wood ever leaves." She looked soberly into Meg's face. "Poor *My-*

fanwy," she said. "It is you I pity, not your two friends. For know this: if you would save yourself this night, you will by this lose yourself, and you will stay lost for the rest of your days."

"What do you mean?" Meg asked, pricked to tears. Greylen had called her by her true name.

Greylen once more shook her head. "Your ears are closed, child. You would not understand."

Would not understand? Under her tears, Meg was stung. *Would not understand,* the woman said, and that after using Meg's proper Welsh name, Gran Jenkins's name, which meant my fine one! "Try me," she said.

"Perhaps I will," Greylen answered her, "even though time is short. Tell me of your Morgan le Fay, Meg-Wilson, if you will."

Morgan le Fay? Meg looked puzzled. What did that have to do with anything? "She is—*was* a witch queen—not like Samana, you said. But not like you, either. She was Welsh, you know. Celtic, like me. And my mother. And Gran Jenkins. Gran Jenkins reads the tarot cards and tells fortunes. She has the second sight." She stopped. "That's what you meant when you said I had the power, isn't it? That's the difference between Sue and me."

Greylen nodded. "Now are *you* the clever one. Sue's is a young spirit, as yet untried. But yours, Meg-Wilson, goes back to the times beyond your country's history books. Please continue your account of Morgan le Fay."

For a moment, Meg was of a mind to take the pathstone and go, but the invitation was irresistible.

"People think of her as bad. They say that she tried to murder her brother, King Arthur of the Round Table. And that she also tried to murder her own husband, King Uriens. But she did good things too. She gave Arthur his sword, Excalibur, and, well, when he lay dying, she and two other queens took him onto their barge and bore him from the world to heal his wounds and make him whole again. It was '. . . *a dusky barge, Dark as a funeral scarf from stem to stern,'* and the three queens wore *'crowns of gold.'*

> *. . . and from them rose*
> *A cry that shiver'd to the tingling stars,*
> *And, as it were one voice, an agony,*
> *Of lamentation, like a wind, that shrills*
> *All night in a waste land, where no one*
> *   comes,*
> *Or hath come, since the making of the*
> *   world . . .*

"That's Alfred Lord Tennyson. We learned it in school last year. Isn't it good? You'd almost think he'd been there!"

Greylen smiled. "Very good. You like this Morgan le Fay very much; it is clear."

From behind them, Sue made a little choking sound.

"I know more than that," Meg went on quickly. "She is also called *Nimue*, and *Vivian*, but those names are wrong, too. Her true name goes right back to the Mabinogion—that's a *really* old collection of Welsh bardic tales. Her real name is *Rhiannon*, and she was wed to King Pwyll. And some say *he* wed her pretending to be Annwyn, King of Darkness, when she had really been promised to Gwawl, King of Light."

"Ah, yes. The riddle of Rhiannon: darkness and light." Greylen nodded. "And still it plagues us all."

"I don't get you," Meg said.

"Inside us all, the powers of darkness and light constantly fight to have their way. I suppose that in your sixth grade class, you'd call it the battle between our good and bad sides. Rhiannon's good and bad sides were *so* strong, and there were so very many shades in between."

Meg's mouth dropped open. "You speak as though you knew her personally."

"Oh, yes, Meg-Wilson. For she belonged not entirely to your world." Greylen sighed. "So many tales you now tell of her in so many dif-

108

ferent countries, and all contradicting one another. How much truth is there really in any of them? And how much does it matter now? So deep was she that no one ever knew her properly. Meg-Wilson, there were not *three* queens upon that funeral barge, but only one, and that was Rhiannon, your Morgan le Fay. The other two, in their black veils and golden crowns, were only phantoms of her other selves. I know this because I was there."

"You were *there?* At the death of *King Arthur?*" Meg was overcome.

"But as for you, child," Greylen went on, "this is strong stuff, this body of legend that you would take to yourself. And you have been badly burned."

Burned? Meg looked down involuntarily at her hands.

"You have looked at Rhiannon, and in her you have seen yourself—only the good side, of course."

"Of course."

"But without your knowing it, Meg-Wilson, the more you have defended her, the more have you hidden from the truth. Child—you have not taken Morgan le Fay's good side to yourself, but her bad one. Deep in your heart—and so deep that you will not admit it even to yourself—you see yourself, and her, as a destroyer, one that kills, one that betrays.

"But even that side you have read wrongly. Morgan le Fay was not a destroyer, but rather a challenger. Always would she test the truth and strength of those who would rule over others. In the fierce flame of her power was assayed the mettle of kings. Think on this, child, and perhaps then you will come to hate yourself less."

Meg's face flamed as though she had been slapped.

How dare Greylen say that! How dare she! She *didn't* think that Morgan le Fay was bad. After all the trouble Meg had taken to stress how wonderful she was, and how much she admired her! But then Meg remembered how she had mistaken Samana for Morgan le Fay. She had been upset at the time, but she had accepted it all the same. Then she also remembered Kenny's words earlier:

You don't like nobody, and nobody likes you. . . . They say you don't even like yourself!

Fresh tears pricked her eyes. "What you say is not true," she said. "Not any of it. Not about me and how I feel about Morgan le Fay. You just don't understand!"

Fifteen

She did not even say goodbye.
She just turned from Greylen and
walked away. On she went, walking blindly past
the birch clumps and through the puddles of
moonlight. The moon had risen higher, making
everything in the clearing look brighter, making the darkness beyond look darker and more
forbidding.

Suddenly, she did not want to go.

She slowed and turned.

Sue had not followed her. She was all alone.

Where was that girl?

There she came in a rush, puffing and panting. Meg watched her resentfully. Greylen had said Sue had brains. And courage. Had she implied by comparison that she, Meg, hadn't any?

"Come *on!*" she called. "We haven't all night!"

"I'm coming, I'm coming." Poor Sue. She couldn't go any faster.

Meg took one last look at the little clearing, then it was lost from sight. As they passed from light to dark, her spirits fell. She wished now that she hadn't left without saying goodbye. Oh, well, too bad. She was always doing things like that and feeling sorry about them afterward.

"Meg . . ."

"Quiet." *Now where,* she muttered to herself.

"Why aren't you using the pathstone?" Sue asked her. She would. Sue always told her to do things just as she was about to do them. Meg weighed the stone in her hand.

"Meg . . ."

"I said, quiet. I'm trying to think."

"I was late because Greylen told me something else."

"If it's about those boys, forget it." She squinted down at the pathstone.

"But I think—"

"Don't." Meg felt it squirm slightly.

"—that you should listen," Sue said.

"Make it quick." There, the stone pointed that way. The moon would be directly at their backs.

"She said," Sue lowered her voice, "that folk who didn't get out of here before dawn never got out at all."

"What did she say happened to them?"

"She said . . . that Queen Samana kept them for the lean times."

"Lean times?"

"The times when nobody comes into the Wood on Halloween."

"Oh, golly! Now she tells me! Let's get going, then. We don't know how far we have to go yet!" In her haste, she dropped the pathstone. "Now look what you've made me do! You *oaf!*"

She scrambled about on her hands and knees, rummaging in the leaves under a log.

"Here, let me," Sue said, dropping down beside her. "You're only making it worse."

"Oh, keep your big feet out of the way. You

couldn't even find yourself in your own back-yard!"

She heard the words, knew she shouldn't have said them, but she was so upset and tired and fussed that she couldn't stop herself.

It was no good. She squealed as her fingers touched something cold and wiggly. She jumped up and started running. She'd never find the pathstone in all that muck. Greylen would just have to lend them another. She ran a little way, then some more, and some more. All was dark and overgrown like the rest of the Wood. The birch clearing, Greylen, Greylen's six "friends," and the Three Sisters were all gone.

Sobbing now, she stumbled back to Sue, who was still sitting where she had left her.

"Get up, stupid," she cried. "Don't you care what happens to us?"

"I certainly do, and that's why I'm still down here." Sue held out the pathstone. "It was just where you dropped it, Meg. If we'd both gone off, we'd never have found this spot again."

Meg took the stone without comment and cupped it in her palm. If Sue thought she was going to eat humble pie she could think again. But she had to admit that Greylen had been right. The girl was smart—oh, bother Sue and her brains!

Meg peered down at the stone. "This way." She began to lead them on.

"But Meg, don't you think we should—"

"If it's about the boys, no."

"But Greylen said—"

Meg stopped and turned. "I don't give a fig what Greylen said. It's all very fine for her sitting back in her clearing—or wherever she is right now. You saw Samana and all those awful creatures. If Greylen can't go against them, what chance have we? Now I don't want to hear any more, all right?"

Sue did not answer.

As they went on in silence, Meg tried to keep the image of the cottage in her mind, and, to be on the safe side, the image of Mother Baldry in it, stirring her stew. But, strangely, the image of the Spike kept intruding, which was distracting. The last thing she wanted them to do was to bump into him!

And then, also, thoughts of Kenny and Rip got in the way no matter how hard she tried to keep them out: Rip lying on that black slab with those awful Mummers circling him and Samana raising the skull to strike; Kenny lying face down where the Spike had felled him with his dreamstick. And every time she thought of them, the pathstone would wiggle, go off course, and she had to stop and take their bearings again.

On they went, and on.

The minutes felt like hours—maybe they were hours. How could they know, climbing up and down through bush and creeper and cold, swampy places where little streams choked with fallen leaves had overflowed their banks.

It was not easy, even with the pathstone.

"We're never going to make it," Meg said at last. "This place just goes on and on. I think it shifts about, somehow. I—"

"Look!" cried Sue.

Meg looked.

There, just a little way in front, was a break in the trees. And beyond that was the cottage.

She did have one moment's doubt.

Poor Myfanwy. It is you I pity, not your two friends. . . .

Then she pushed the words from her mind and began to run.

"Whoopee!" Meg cried. "We did it! Come on, Sue, come on!"

And she ran out, out from the dark trees, leaving the Wood behind.

Sixteen

She was about five paces from the door when she faltered. Sue ran right into her.

"What is it, Meg?"

"I can't."

"Can't?"

"Can't go through with it, what do you think?" Tears prickled her eyes. By now out there, just a few yards away, Mother and Father and probably the entire Locust Valley police force were looking for them . . . and for Kenny, and Rip. When they were through, what would she say to Mother? . . . to Kenny's mother?

To herself?

Oh, *bother* Greylen, and those boys!

But even if she did turn back, it was too late to help them now. The tears came fast.

"Meg, Meg, what is it?"

"Oh, shut up. You know very well."

She turned from Sue, who said, "It's not yet eleven-thirty, Meg. I can just see my watch."

Meg rounded on her, venting the full force of her shame and regret. "It's no use, don't you see? Those things that Greylen had. I didn't take them. So there's no point in going back."

"But there is, Meg. Here." Sue held out her hand.

In it were the glass phial and the little glass ball.

"Greylen gave them to me as we left. Just in case you changed your mind, she said. She made me promise not to say a word unless you asked for them."

Meg burst into tears. "Oh, Sue, Sue."

Sue patted her shoulder awkwardly. "There, there. It's all right."

Meg coughed, sniffed, took out her hanky and blew her nose.

All right? Of course it was all right! She was going back to get that awfully slobby boy and his runty brother, so help her, or her name wasn't . . . Myfanwy.

She took the phial and the globe from Sue's outstretched hand and stowed them in her jeans' back pocket.

"Right, now. First we think of Kenny by the rock."

Resolutely, she turned her back on the cottage, on the little lighted window, on the sliver of yellow light shining from under the closed door, to face once more the gloomy menace of the wood. Refusing to waste any more time thinking of their parents and the safety they were leaving behind, Meg walked forward, filling her mind with thoughts of Kenny: of Kenny swaggering to the edge of the clearing; Kenny saying, *It's prob'ly nothing but an old racoon;* Kenny falling under the Spike's dreamstick.

It didn't take many steps before they lost sight of the cottage. All too soon, the darkness wrapped them up.

What if the Spike finds you and touches you with the dreamstick? What then? And what if—what if Samana finds you first?

She shook those fears from her mind over and over, thinking of Kenny, Kenny, Kenny.

The stone twisted and turned about.

It did not take long to reach him. He had not moved. He looked so cold lying there. When he awoke, he would be very stiff, Meg thought, kneeling down beside him. What an awkward position he had fallen into, with his left arm pinned under him and his knee bent up like that. His clothes were soaked in dew. Meg sighed. There was nothing they could do about that. By now their clothes were in even worse condition than any of Kenny's.

She was just loosing the stopper on the phial when Sue whispered, "Someone's coming."

Meg didn't argue.

Quickly, they dodged back behind the rock.

Out of the darkness came the Spike, followed by the two bearers, their stark white masks gleaming like disembodied faces floating through the trees. Without a word, they picked Kenny up, laid him on the litter, and began to carry him off.

"Oh, how ghastly!" Meg realized that there was only black space where their hands should be.

Sue's breath tickled her ear. "Where are they taking him?"

"I don't know. Samana has her sacrifice for tonight. Perhaps she's having him taken to the cavern." *To keep him for the lean times* . . .

Sue nodded. "What do we do now?"

"Follow them. What else can we do? Come on."

They followed the Spike and the bearers for a long time until they came to the foot of a steep slope—a cliff, really—much higher and darker and more forbidding than the one in the birch clearing.

At last the Spike and the bearers stopped before a narrow cleft in the rocks, which they entered. Meg grabbed Sue and followed. The cleft widened into a passage, then arched over their heads to form a tunnel.

The Spike took down a torch from the wall, carrying it high in front of him to light the way. Its flames threw grotesque shadows behind him, like long fingers ordering her to go back, Meg thought.

They went on, along a maze of passages, round and round and down until they came out at last into the vault of the high cavern that they had seen pictured over the white stone. Meg's nose pinched in distaste. It was the stink of the ruined cottage all over again.

The Spike had the bearers set the litter down

by the purple wall behind the queen's throne;
then he waved them out. When they had gone,
he took off his helmet to scratch his head, and
for the first time, Meg saw his face.

It was not at all what she had expected.

It was blunt, rather full and hearty, and
somehow quite familiar. Now where had she
seen it before?

He bent over to fuss with Kenny, straighten-
ing him up, crossing his arms neatly over
his chest.

Just as though Kenny were dead already, Meg
thought in disgust.

Beside her, Sue whispered, "It's Tom Baldry.
Mother Baldry's boy!"

The words carried much further than they
should have.

The Spike looked up. "Who's there!"

Crouched behind their rock pillar, Meg and
Sue went very stiff.

The Spike got to his feet and strode over.

"Here! Come on out! Come on—*out!*"

There was a pause, and when still they didn't
move, he reached down to his belt, drew out his
dreamstick, and raised his arm to strike.

Seventeen

Meg stood up slowly, just out of reach. After a moment's hesitation, Sue got up too, right behind her.

"Hoho—now I remember you—you are the two that ran off. I was hoping that you wouldn't show up again."

Meg relaxed enough to take her eyes off the stick for a quick glance at his face. Yes, she could see now the round, jolly features of the old woman in the cottage.

"Hey—" The Spike, alias Tom Baldry, was staring at them. "How come you knew my name?"

"Your mother told us," Meg said stoutly, sounding braver than she felt.

"My . . . *mother?*" Tom looked stunned. "How—where did you see her?"

"In your house. Where else? She gave us some very good stew. And she told us to tell you, quote, his poor ma's keeping the lamp lit and the pot hot, and to hurry on home, unquote."

"Quote, unquote?" Tom looked doubtful.

"Those were her exact words, Tom."

"Oh, I see." The smiley lines in his homely face drooped, leaving it unutterably sad.

"She also said that you were, quote, *a good boy*, unquote, and that there wasn't the match of you anywhere."

"She said that?" A tear started down the side of his nose.

He tucked the dreamstick back in his belt and squatted beside them. "After all the trouble I caused her." He shook his head sadly.

"What trouble?" Meg asked.

Tom sighed. "The usual. Me and Mike Smith and Timmy Ogden went out drinking again, after I promised her solemn I wouldn't no more. We got back late on account of Timmy losing his horse, and we went down to the crick to sober up. On the way back, we met *her*. Mike managed to get away, but I'll lay a bet he never told what happened. She took Timmy that night, poor beggar. Me, she set aside. For a lean year, she said. But she never took me. There's something about me that won't 'take.' I heard her talking to her critter about me one time. But there's worse she can do with a body than take him, I tell you. And sometimes it's more than flesh and blood can stand."

Meg nodded, eyeing him up and down. Tom had plenty of both.

"So she made me her lootenant. Gave me this here gear to wear—it ain't no Yankee getup, that's for sure—and this here stick." Tom laughed cheerlessly.

"Yes, we've seen you use it," Meg said, edging away a bit, but not enough to make a federal case out of it.

"I don't like the work, and that's a fact," Tom went on. "Each year I swear I'll not do it no more, but what choice have I got? It's either them"—he nodded to Kenny asleep on the litter—"or me. It's the very little ones that bother me the most."

"What are you going to do with the boy?" Meg asked Tom.

Tom stood up, towering over them. "Leave him here for her. I had to get him, you understand? She sent me special."

He put his helmet back on, and at once Meg began to feel afraid. The homely Tom was gone, and the awful Spike was back in his place. "And us? What will you do with us?"

"Nothing—for now. But she's heard of you from others, just like with this one." He stood over them, considering. "You say my ma gave you hot pot. Was it good?"

"Oh, yes," Sue said. "It was lovely. Hot. And hearty . . . you know."

Tom looked wistful. "Yes, I know. Tell you what: if I let you go, will you take her a message from me?"

Meg and Sue nodded energetically.

"Tell her that I'm on a job right now, but not to worry, I'll be home when it's done."

Another tear strayed off the end of his nose.

Meg got to her feet, still careful to stay out of reach.

"We'll do that," she said.

"Promise?"

"Promise."

"All right, then. You can go, and I'm obliged.

But this one stays." He nudged Kenny with his boot. "I can't afford that much trouble, you understand?"

Meg nodded, trying to hide her growing impatience.

Tom walked them out of the cavern and back up through the maze of passages. Outside, he parted from them with directions, warnings, and much advice.

"And when you get there, you won't let on about what I'm really doing these days, will you? Just give her a big kiss, and tell her not to give up."

Tom's tears were flowing freely now.

Meg took out her hanky and handed it over. "Here. Keep it."

Tom took it, shook it, then blew his nose loudly.

"Well, if I don't go I'll be late, and then I'll catch it," he said. "Goodbye, and take care. It's been nice talking."

He'd gone but a little way when he stopped and looked back.

"No hard feelings about your friends?"

Meg shrugged. "They're no friends of ours."

No sooner was he out of sight than they ran back to the shadow of the cliff. Meg stopped. They would not get very far in that maze and certainly not without light. She took the little glass ball from her pocket and squeezed it in her right hand.

"If this glass ball can stall Samana, then maybe it can give us some light." She closed her eyes, and pictured herself as the Statue of Liberty with the flaming torch in her hand.

"Oh, Meg—it works!" Sue cried.

Sure enough, the little glass ball was glowing, not brightly, but enough to show the way the pathstone pointed.

It was not easy, going back up that jumble of crisscrossing tunnels, to keep the light lit and the pathstone pointing in the right direction. "I feel like a juggler," Meg grumbled, but underneath she couldn't help feeling proud of herself.

At last they came out into the high cavern where Kenny still lay under the garish light behind Samana's throne.

"It does suit him, though," Meg remarked, kneeling down again and twisting out the stopper of the little phial.

"What does?"

"That ghastly purple. Can't you see him in that arcade at Roosevelt, zinging and popping and whatever else they do in there." Oh, boy, there you go again, she told herself. Kenny was right. You are a snob.

Three drops, Greylen said. She must be sure

to leave enough for Rip. Gingerly, she pulled down Kenny's lower lip and dripped three drops down the inside of his cheek. Ugh. How she would hate to be a nurse. She wiped her hand on the back of her jeans and sealed up the phial again.

At first, nothing happened. Sue took up Kenny's hands and began to chafe them.

Kenny stirred, opened his eyes, and made a queer grunting sound.

"Oh, dear," Sue said. "I don't like it, Meg. Something's wrong."

"Wrong?" Kenny tried to sit up. "What's wrong? Can't a guy wake up in peace?" He looked around and began to focus. "Hey . . . what're we doing? Where is this?" He looked around again, wincing. "Where's Rip?"

"Can you stand up, Kenny?" Meg said.

Kenny came up in painful stages, groaning all the way.

"Hey—level with me. What's been going on? Where's the kid?"

"Well, to tell the truth, Kenny, he's been, er, snatched."

"Snatched? What do you mean, *snatched*?"

"I mean he's in trouble, and we're in trouble, and if you want him back we have to move— fast!"

"Now wait a minute—"

"Kenny," Meg repeated firmly, "I said, fast."

"Okay, okay, *okay!*" Kenny raised his hands in mock defense, then added, "This had better be good, Wilson, and not just a cheap shot to pay me back."

"It is and it isn't, and Sue will tell you all about it on the way. Let's go."

"But where? Where are we going?" Kenny said. She heard Sue hush him up, vaguely heard their whispering as they moved out of the cavern into the passages, heard his exclamation as she lit up the little glass ball and held it over her head to light their way out again, but soon she was concentrating too hard to pay them much attention.

When at last they emerged into the open, Meg doused the little globe—just by thinking it dark again—and they moved on toward the deep hollow.

Meg remembered the cold of that place and how it had sapped her will.

I don't care what happens, nobody, but nobody will ever get me to go down there again!

Well, here she was, about to do that very thing.

The question was, would she get out again this time?

Eighteen

As the ground began to dip, Meg stopped.

"We are close. From now on, speak only if you must."

"Just a sec." Kenny took her arm. "Exactly who's in charge? If you think Kenny Stover's taking any more orders from a girl—you're crazy."

"Now look here . . ." Meg began ominously.

"Do you know," Sue said, coming between them, "that my sister and I could have been home by now? We actually made the cottage—close enough to touch it—but Meg came back for you. If it weren't for her, you'd still be lying back there. And furthermore, Kenny Stover," she persisted, as Kenny tried to speak, "Meg knows what to do, and Greylen says she's the only one that can do it. So if you want Rip back, listen to her, and listen *good!*"

Meg stared at Sue in surprise.

"Oh wow," Kenny said, and shut up.

Meg led them on, on and down. Presently, she stopped again. She could feel the cold pressing in on her and could sense the evil growing stronger. "Kenny, do you feel any different?"

"How—*different*?"

"Sleepy. Spooky. Scared."

Kenny squared his shoulders.

"Kenny Stover's scared of nothing and nobody," he said.

"Suit yourself," Meg said. She went on again, following the twisting stone, tracing its angle in her palm with her free hand, scarce able to see it now. And all the while, the fear in her grew until she began to feel that the very trees around them were watching their every step.

When they reached the clearing, it was deserted.

"Hey," Kenny said. "I don't like this." He sounded subdued. "Where's Rip? I thought you said the kid would be here."

Meg ignored him, beginning to realize what a nuisance she must have been to Greylen. She took out the little globe and squeezed it in her hand. If she tried hard enough, it would show her what she needed to see, or so Greylen had said.

And what she needed to see was the baddies: to determine whether they were coming or going—to learn whether she and Sue and Kenny were not too late.

She opened up her hand and stared into the ball. It began to glow with a milky light; then it cleared, and tiny images moved about inside it like reflections caught in a fish-eye lens.

There they were, the leech things, and the brown-and-purple Leapers, and the dead-alive folk moving slowly, so slowly, down, down, in a snaky line, each holding onto the waist of the one in front, in and out of the trees. They were doing a dance, a ghastly farandole, that they probably did at this time every year.

Down! They were still coming down! She was in time—but only just.

"They're coming," she said. "Quick—where can we hide?"

Kenny found a large pile of boulders with a

space at its center large enough for them all to crawl into. It was set back from the clearing, but near enough for them to see the slab.

Reluctantly, Kenny squeezed in first. Then Sue. Then Meg. It was a tight fit and an uncomfortable one. Meg was glad that Sue was in the middle. She would have been embarrassed to be squashed so closely against Kenny, even in the fix they were in.

"It's very close in here," Sue said.

"At least it's warm." Kenny laughed, a rough laugh, dry and coarse. Meg had grown to hate that laugh, for mostly it had been directed against her. But just then she welcomed the sound, for it reminded her of the outside, everyday world.

Meg stared out into the empty clearing and seeing the black slab, she shivered. That place was like the arena where the old Christian martyrs were thrown to the lions . . . only worse, much worse.

Just then, she caught a slight movement in the bushes to her left. Yes, there it was, just as she had seen it in the holograph: the first leech-creature coming out from the trees. Another came, then another, and another.

In came the brown-and-purple Leapers through the high branches, then the multitude.

Kenny squirmed past Sue to take a look.

"Oh, my," he said. And, "Wow."

Meg shifted uneasily. It was all happening just as it had above the white stone, only now it was real, and happening live—

Her eyelids drooped. Oh, no. She was beginning to doze off. But she must not; she must not. She shifted position, becoming aware then that Kenny and Sue were no longer jostling for the better view.

"Sue?" There was no reply. "Kenny?" He did not answer either. Meg's throat felt prickly and dry. Whatever had to be done, she would have to do alone. The only trouble was the funny buzzing in her head, a gentle, soothing noise. How nice it would be, she thought, just to lie there and sleep . . .

Behind the buzzing in her head, a voice cried, *Meg-Wilson—awake!*

Her eyelids fluttered. That voice was familiar. It was the same one that had disturbed her the last time she was down here.

Greylen's voice.

She might have guessed.

Her eyes closed again.

Wake up, child! It is your will and power that must carry the day! Stir yourself! Open your eyes! What do you see?

Meg half-opened her eyes and peered out.

I see the Three Mummers. They are circling the slab. They've got those funny sticks in their hands and all that stuff on their heads. She tried to think. What were they? Oh, yes. Mandragora, the ceiba tree, and . . . and . . . She couldn't think.

The fungus, Meg-Wilson, remember? The fungus.

Meg nodded drowsily. Oh, yes. Stinkhorn. In the hand. On the head. Oh, if only she didn't have to stay awake . . .

Hold, Meg-Wilson! Tell me what you now see!

Mildly irritated, Meg looked out again. *I see the Craven.*

She yawned as it approached the slab.

Meg-Wilson—child!

Meg scowled. Why couldn't Greylen leave her be?

Raise your head. Do not let yourself be overcome. Hold fast! You must stay alert if you are to prevail!

Prevail? Meg pulled her hand out of her pocket and felt the tiny globe humming in her palm. How strange. It was vibrating like the little massage cushion she'd bought Father for his birthday. She transferred it to her other hand, let it tingle that one too. Wasn't she supposed to be doing something with it?

Not yet. You must choose the time exactly, right on the stroke of midnight. Not a moment early, not a moment late.

But I haven't a watch.

There was no reply. Was Greylen offended? Watch. She needed a watch.

"Sue," she murmured sleepily. Sue had a watch. Must see . . . watch. She took Sue's limp wrist, groped for the watch dial, and raised it to her face. Of course, she couldn't see a thing. *Can't*, she told Greylen. *Won't know the time. Too dark to see.* Now maybe Greylen would leave her in peace.

In came the ghastly bearers with Rip, followed by the Spike. No—it was Tom, wasn't it? Tom Baldry. She vaguely recalled having met his mother somewhere . . .

Meg-Wilson. The voice was urgent now. *It is time!*

She could no longer move.

Myfanwy! Awake!

Awake? Time?

Time!

Her eyelids flicked open wide.

She remembered the round white stone in the little cave and, above it, the holograph Rip lying on the black slab. She saw again the Dark Queen's arm raised above him, the yellow skull . . .

And now came Samana, the real Samana, life-size, sweeping in over the heads of all those people, those poor, lost people, lost . . .

Lost!

Samana had come for Rip!

She put her hands over her face. She squeezed her eyes shut against the memory of what she had seen. She could not watch that awful skull descend onto Rip's head, could not watch that abominable thing hop up and—she must do something.

But I can't, she told herself.

The little globe burned in her hand, stinging her, bringing her mind to a single point.

Yes, I can, she said. I must. I have no choice . . .

Samana shall not have her way this night!

The words growled through her head. Whose words were they? Greylen's? Or her own? Did it matter? She scrambled up and out from beneath the rock pile, and edged forward into the throng.

Nineteen

There had been no sound back in Greylen's cave, but there was plenty of it here, and it was ugly and wild. Samana whirled about the slab, faster and faster. Meg craned her neck to watch.

Abruptly, Samana turned and gestured to Tom to fetch the skull.

Meg edged out into the middle of the crowd,

trying not to feel the horror of its deadness as the Dark Queen held out her hand for the head of Goga and the Three Mummers went through their horrid rite.

Snatching the skull, Samana raised it high above her head and circled the slab.

As in the holograph, hands reached out for it and her.

The racket was appalling.

Seconds to go.

She must do something.

What?

She must not let that thing descend onto Rip's forehead.

She was wide awake now.

What could she do?

Only if your will be strong . . .

The words went round and round in her head.

She had wanted light, and that tiny globe had lit her way.

She had wanted to see where the baddies were, and it had shown them to her.

Now what did she want?

She wanted . . . she wanted somehow to surprise Samana for that one precious second when her powers would be at their height.

But how?

Meg thought quickly. She herself could not

stop Samana. So who could? Who would the Dark Queen least expect to see in this, her strongest hour? Why, Greylen, of course. What a shock it would be for Samana to see the Birch Queen there, not only in the clearing—but on the slab itself!

Meg stared down at the little ball in her hand, willing with all her might, as Samana, shrieking, rushed up to the slab and raised the skull.

The shriek changed abruptly into a screech as suddenly, upon the altar beside Rip's head, Queen Greylen appeared, shining like a star—the Birch Queen, who should have been at home in her glade.

The crowd was hushed.

Inside that shining light that looked like Greylen, Meg stood on that terrible slab, feeling its cold sucking the very strength from her, feeling her will falter. The light was fading, she was sure. She looked down. Rip's face was chalk white in the glow of her radiance. Strength surged through her then, and her will hardened. No, not her will alone, but the combined will of all of Greylen's people: the women in their garlands, the Three Sisters in their little cave, and Greylen herself. Can they see me now, Meg wondered. Is my image shining above the white stone?

What a long moment it was. It felt as though time itself had stopped.

Samana snarled, gestured the Craven up onto the slab. For a moment, Meg thought it would refuse, but then it hopped up to perch beside Rip's feet, well clear of Meg.

Samana raised the skull again.

What now? She had nothing left with which to hold the Dark Queen at bay. Except . . .

The tiny globe flashed in her left hand, and in her right appeared a shining staff, as solid as the handle of a hockey stick.

The Craven flopped off the end of the slab and away.

Samana went still, the skull suspended above her head. Then, with an angry cry that resounded through the silence, she threw it down and flew off into the trees.

Rejoice! The hour is past! Clear voices exulted in Meg's ear.

At once the clearing filled with terrifying, inhuman sounds of wailing and groaning and howling, as the multitude scattered away into the trees.

She stood alone on the slab. The staff was gone. Had it, too, been but an illusion?

No. It was truly mine own, at its full power in your hand. And that power was yours, Meg-

Wilson, and you would save your own! Never before has there been such a thing! Samana is badly thrown! But not for long. She has gone to fetch her warstaff. Get down, child. Take your friend and go!

Meg jumped down and tried to lift Rip from the litter, but her knees were shaking, and her strength was gone. The light had quite faded from her now, and she was plain Meg again.

Oh, give me strength, she sobbed, not thinking of the globe at all. No sooner had she thought it, than she was able to lift Rip as easily as if she had been Kenny. Kenny! And Sue! Where were they?

She turned to see them running through the empty clearing toward her. "Oh, Meg, Meg!" Sue cried. She put her arms about Meg and squeezed her tight.

"Here, mind Rip," Meg said. "You're squashing him."

Kenny took his brother from Meg's arms, and hoisted him over his shoulder.

"You were wonderful!" Sue hugged Meg again, jogging her up and down. "I didn't know it was you. Kenny wanted to rush out, but I told him to stay put. I thought you were really Greylen, you see. It looked so scary, you and Samana standing there, face to face. I thought—"

"No time to think, Sue. Let's go!"

They began to scramble back the way they had come, up the side of the hollow.

"We'll have to watch out," Meg said over her shoulder. "Those things must be all over the—"

Sue screamed. "Meg!"

Ahead, the Craven blocked Meg's path. Before she could think, it reached out a wing and knocked her to her knees. Meg remembered the sharp beak opened wide over Rip in the cavern and squeezed her eyes shut, bracing herself for the pain that was surely to come.

But it didn't.

She opened her eyes to find the Craven lying beside her. Above it stood Tom Baldry, minus helmet. In his fist was the dreamstick.

'The times I've wanted to do that," he said. "Here." He reached for Meg's hand, pulling her to her feet. "Come on, for *she's* on her way, and what she isn't going to do to you when she catches you. She's onto you, you know." He turned to Kenny. "Here. Give us that lad." Tom reached for Rip.

"No way." Kenny retreated from him.

"It's all right," Sue said. "It's Tom, Mother Baldry's boy. He saw Meg and me before and never gave us away. And you saw just now how he saved Meg from that awful bird-thing."

"That's right," Tom said. "So if you want to move quick, just hand him over and follow me."

"Back to your mother's house, Tom?" Meg asked.

"Aye. 'Tis the only way. Of course, I won't see it. All I ever see when I go that way—which is often enough—is a kind of mist that I can't ever reach."

From below them came an enraged shout.

"We'd best be moving," Tom said, hitching Rip over his shoulder much as Kenny had done. "And don't give way. Tell yourselves that every passing minute is on your side. Come on."

They slipped and slid and clawed their way out of the hollow.

From time to time Meg thought she saw vague shadows near where they passed, but no one challenged them.

"They're leaving you for her," Tom said.

Once, though, a brawny pirate with a braid down his back took hold of Sue's arm and would have pulled her away had not Tom felled him with the dreamstick.

"Not far now," Tom said, wheezing loudly. "Funny. I had expected her to catch up with us by now."

"What about you, Tom?" It hurt Meg's throat to speak. "What will Samana do when she finds out that you helped us?"

"Do?" Tom considered. "Oh, I'll worry about that when the time comes. But—don't tell Ma, will you? She'll worry so."

"We won't." Meg trotted alongside him. "We promised."

Sue spoke up from behind. "You can come with us, if you want, Tom."

"If I—" Tom stopped. "Now, missy—that's unkind."

"But you can!" Sue's voice rose. "Greylen told me that if Samana should miss a sacrifice, one person would get freed. And that's you, Tom. Greylen meant you. She knew you'd help us."

Tom went on again, shaking his massive head. "No," he said. "No one ever leaves this place. No one."

"Oh, yes they do. We're leaving, and so are you. Greylen said. And she wouldn't lie."

"Maybe she wouldn't at that." Tom speeded up again. "Tell you what: the cottage is just ahead. If I see mist, you're wrong, and—"

"—and if you see the cottage, she's right!" Meg cried, joining in.

A moment later, Tom shouted.

"It's the cottage! There's the light in the window, as clear as day! It's true! I'm free! Look out, Ma, here I come!"

At that moment, something swept out of the

trees and an icy wind brushed past. Tom threw up his arms over Meg's head to protect her and was swept off his feet.

There was a roaring and a tumult as, in passing, the wind whipped the forest floor and filled the air with choking debris.

"It's *her!*" Tom cried. "She's not going to let you through! Go for the light! See it? Go! Go for your lives!"

Twenty

Kenny seized Rip and staggered toward the homely cottage door. Whereas it had been closed that last time, it was now open wide, and through the murk Meg saw the lamplight spilling out, forming a path of gold.

Stoutly framed in the doorway and partially

blocking that bright path was Mother Baldry, peering out blindly toward her son.

Times I've gone over to that door to put on my coat and go out to look for him, but somehow something's always gotten in my way.

Time . . . Time was blurring again, and overlapping at its edges . . .

Time. . . . Even in that quick second, Meg looked at the open door and knew. She and Sue had not been meant to go through before. That was why it had been closed.

Now it was fully open—but for whom?

Kenny was halfway there, Sue not far behind. Meg started after them, then stopped and turned as the icewind bore down again.

Tom was still lying where he had fallen, numb from Samana's touch. "Go!" he called again. "You're a brave lass, but that shouldn't make you a fool!"

"No, Tom. I'll not leave you to that horrid old hag."

"That's no talk for a young lady," said Tom, then he shouted a warning as the wind current swept the path and Samana stood squarely between Meg and the cottage door.

Not one word did she speak, but only looked— that same look she'd given Meg from over the white stone.

Meg's knees began to give way. She remembered Gran Jenkins saying, "Where there is a will there is a way."

Behind Samana, the figures of Sue and Kenny and Rip wavered, then disappeared behind Mother Baldry's bulk. Well, they were safe, anyhow.

Meg pressed the little ball in the palm of her hand.

Now who could she be? The Greylen image wouldn't work a second time. Who, then? Who could stand against Samana now?

All at once, it came to her. And having chosen, she willed and willed until she felt herself growing taller, taller, and shining with a terrible light. She pulled herself up, her eyes wide, her hands filling with power, ancient power drawn from a world even before Samana's time.

Samana snarled, and raised her hands on high. Light forked from them to strike Meg and Tom, but in that moment Meg was not Meg but someone wonderful and awful and strong—and out to save her own.

Like Samana, she was; yet unlike, there being in her humanity—for hadn't she, who had once tried to destroy her brother, King Arthur, also taken him to her to heal his wounds and end his pain?

There was no one, *no one*, thought Meg, to equal Morgan le Fay.

Tom ducked.

Meg-Wilson-Morgan-le-Fay reached out. She caught the light that had come from Samana, and hurled it back at her. Samana went forward to lay hands on Meg, but Meg burned now with an anger fierce enough to set the whole Wood afire.

Forward she advanced, Tom at her heels, and forward, until she and the Dark Queen were face to face.

I mustn't waver, Meg told herself sternly. If I weaken once, all will be lost. She looked into Samana's eyes, the eyes that had so cowed her back in the little cave. She saw the evil therein, and the cruelty, and the need to crush and destroy.

But you'll not destroy me, Meg's eyes said back. You can't. Because I'm not like you. And I never will be.

She stepped forward again, and this time Samana stepped back.

Then Meg-Wilson-Morgan-le-Fay raised *her*

arms and sent out a stream of light that touched the air around her with blue fire. Out it spread until the edge of it reached the Dark Queen.

In an explosion of pain and rage, Samana leapt out of range back into the trees.

"Run!" Meg shouted. "Tom—run!"

Something dark—was it Samana?—shot out at them. Meg, exhausted, stumbled and almost fell, but Tom scooped her up and made for the cottage door.

There was a terrible moment of pain—had Samana clawed her?—then a light, prickling sensation, and they were standing in Mother Baldry's kitchen with the rest.

Rip was lying on the hearth rug, still asleep.

Meg realized that she had one last service to perform—and quickly. Running forward, she knelt down, took the little glass phial from her pocket, and shook its contents into Rip's mouth.

Just as with Kenny, nothing happened at first. Then Rip stirred, stretched, and opened his eyes. At that same moment, as they watched, the phial, the pathstone, and the tiny glass globe all dissolved into the air.

"Well, I never," Mother Baldry said.

What a wonderful mother, Meg thought. Here's her son back after goodness knows how long, and she doesn't even ask him where he's been. She couldn't imagine what their mother was going to say, and after she and Sue had been gone for only a few hours.

Rip looked up wide-eyed from one to the other of them and said, "Kenny, where are we? Who's them?" Then, "Take me home!"

"Why, bless you, I'm not sending you anywhere in that condition, young man," said Mother Baldry. "First, I'll get you cleaned up, and then you shall fill your stomach with a bowl of good, hot stew."

"Well," Kenny said, looking doubtfully at Rip.

Meg laughed. "You might as well, Kenny," she said. "She'll not let you out of here until you have had some."

"Oh, boy," Kenny said, shaking his head. "I don't believe this. I've got to be tripping out."

Meg laughed again. "Welcome to the club," she said.

Mother Baldry bustled about her kitchen, using hot water off the stove to clean their cuts and scratches, then binding them with strips torn from an old sheet smelling of camphor and lavender. Would they still be wearing them when they walked through the front door, Meg wondered, watching the old woman carefully lapping the bindings round and round her arm.

That done, Mother Baldry sat them all around

the table and ladled out her thick brown stew into great blue bowls.

Even Rip stopped his whining long enough to dunk chunks of Mother Baldry's fresh baked bread into the gravy, dribbling it over his chin onto Ken's down vest.

Mother Baldry sat herself contentedly on a stool by the stove to watch them all.

Meg gazed around at the kitchen walls, as though to commit them to memory. *Home Sweet Home,* the sampler said.

Mother in the old sweats that she always wore around the house. Mother looking for her glasses for the umpteenth time. Father in his study bent over his desk in a death lock with his chess machine. And the cats. Did anybody remember to feed them tonight?

"That was the first one I ever sewed," Mother Baldry said. Meg looked at her. "Do you make good stitches?" the old woman asked. "I am sure you do, a young lady like you."

Lady? Meg looked down at her bedraggled clothes and sodden sneakers.

"Her and me," Kenny chipped in, "we do music."

Music? Meg frowned, went quite tense. She saw him again by the apple barrels, his imaginary fiddle on his shoulder, whining in his nose.

She heard his mincing "English" voice: *And now for may grend fee-nah-lee.* After all they had been through, surely he wasn't going back to the old routine . . .

"Yes," Kenny said. "We both play real good—and we tune real good too. She tunes fiddles, and I tune cars."

"Cars?" Mother Baldry looked blank. "That must be a new instrument—is it, Tom? I haven't heard one of them. Do you scrape it, or blow it?"

Kenny stared. Oh, heaven, Meg thought. He still does not realize. . . . She aimed a warning kick at him under the table, but missed.

"So where do you folks live?" Tom held out his bowl for a refill.

"I'm beginning to wonder that myself," Kenny said.

Meg put a hand to her forehead. The excitements of the night were beginning to take effect now in the close warmth of that homely kitchen. She recalled Sue's words when they'd first gone through into the Halloween Wood:

They found a place where there was a hole in the barrier between this time and other times—or was it other worlds?

Sue must have been closer to the truth than she thought, for Meg was now sure that they

155

had done both, via the Baldrys' house—probably because this was where the two worlds—the everyday world and Samana's world—had touched before.

"What year is it?" she asked Tom.

"What year—" Kenny's eyes bugged. "And she calls *me* dumb! It's—ow!" This time Meg's foot found his shin.

"—eighteen-oh-six," Tom said, wiping his mouth on his sleeve. "Ma, this hot pot is one of your best."

"But it isn't eighteen-oh-six anymore, Tom," Mother Baldry corrected him. "That was when you went off. What it is now, I can't rightly say. I seem to have lost count. But I do know that you've been gone pretty long, as I told these young ladies here." She looked fondly into his face. "You still don't look a day older for all that."

"Eighteen-oh-six." Meg held Kenny silent with a look. "Or thereabouts. Of course. How stupid of me to forget."

"Don't worry," Tom said. "I do it all the time. But, say, you still haven't told us where you folks live."

Kenny opened his mouth, closed it again under Meg's eye, and shifted his shins out of range.

Meg considered. It was no good saying 32a Millford Drive, because there was no Millford Drive back in eighteen-oh-six, nor any Horse Hollow Road, nor much of anything save water and trees.

"Well," she said, "it's hard to say, but let's put it this way: wherever *our* house is, *yours* is somewhere between it and—where we found you."

Tom nodded slowly. "I see. Fair enough."

"I surely wish," Mother Baldry spoke up, "that you children came by here more often. I make such good apple pies."

"I'm sure you do, ma'am," Meg said. "And I wish we could, too. But to tell the truth, we live a fair way away. We're only just visiting, you see."

Meg and Sue stood up and quietly slid their chairs under the table. Kenny did likewise, and went around the table for Rip, who had fallen asleep with his head in his arms.

Just like the dormouse in *Alice in Wonderland*, thought Meg. He's done nothing but sleep all night.

She thanked Mother Baldry, said goodbye, and followed Tom down the passage to the front door.

"I hope you young 'uns get home safely," Tom said soberly. "I know there's more to all this than I can understand."

"Oh, I know we will, Tom. Just as soon as we go through that door."

She glanced back up the passage where the others were still saying their goodbyes. Now was the perfect time, the only time she'd have to ask Tom what was uppermost in her mind.

"Tom—what did she look like, out there?"

"Oh!" Tom grinned. "Put out. *Really* put out. I've never seen her *that* mad. It was a treat to see."

"I don't mean Samana, Tom. I mean the other one." Now at last she would know what Morgan le Fay looked like. Why, no one in the whole world knew that!

Tom looked puzzled. "Which other one? There was only the two of you—not counting me."

It was Meg's turn to be at a loss. "I mean— oh, you know how I looked like Greylen back on the black slab? Well, this other one that I turned myself into out there just now—what did she look like? Tom, please try to remember, if you can. She's very important to me."

Tom smiled widely. "And she's very important to me too. And if I stood here to my dying

158

day I still would not have thanked her enough for what she did." He put out a great hand and ruffled her wiry thatch. "Why, it was you, girl. It was you standing there on your own two feet, facing her head on. I couldn't believe my eyes but you whipped her, and whipped her good!"

Meg stared up at him, oblivious of the others coming out into the passage behind her. Her eyes were wide with wonder and a slow smile of pure joy spread across her face.

She had done all that? She couldn't believe it! She, Meg Wilson, had stood against the Dark Queen all by herself—and won! She wanted to leap and shout and laugh and cry, but instead she watched Tom's hand go to the latch.

"And as for you, missy"—Tom looked past Meg to Sue—"if you hadn't told me I could come home, I'd still have been back there. I owe you, too."

"Oh, I don't know," Sue said.

Tom opened the door.

Goodbye, goodbye . . .

One by one they stepped out: Meg, Kenny carrying Rip, and Sue.

One moment they were standing shivering on a little path bright with late roses and fresh with predawn dew, and the next . . .

. . . *goodbye, goodbye . . .*

. . . they stood under the weight of their costumes and masks, the stink of the ruined cottage behind them and the flash of police car lights along the curb ahead. Even Mother Baldry's bandages had disappeared—and so had the injuries. It was almost as if nothing had happened.

Almost.

"Boy." Kenny whistled softly. "Now I'll really catch it. What are we going to say to everybody? Oh, well. See you in school tomorrow, Wilson—if your old man don't ship you back to England on the next plane. I kind of hope he don't."

Meg felt her color rising. "Oh, he won't. I won't let him. I mean . . . well . . . this might not be home, but compared to where we've been tonight, Locust Valley isn't such a very bad place!"